BLOOD In His BOOTS

David Thomasson

iUniverse, Inc.
New York Bloomington

Blood In His Boots

iUniverse books may be ordered through booksellers or by contacting:

iUniverse
1663 Liberty Drive
Bloomington, IN 47403
www.iuniverse.com
1-800-Authors (1-800-288-4677)

ISBN: 978-1-4502-5905-7 (pbk)
ISBN: 978-1-4502-5906-4 (ebk)

Printed in the United States of America

iUniverse rev. date: 10/12/10

The Town of Threeforks, Texas

W
S ←→ N
E

Molly's Boarding House

alley

Rancher's Bank

Three Fork's Bugle Newspaper

alley

dock

Horan's General Store

Silver Spur Saloon

Lindners Blacksmith and Livery

corral

Bessie's Sewing Shop

Western Union

Frontier Hotel

alley

shed

Sheriff's Office

jail

Shorty's Barber Shop

Guns & Saddle Shop

CONTENTS

OUTLINE FOR *BLOOD IN HIS BOOTS*

1. THE SIXTEEN-NOTE HENRY RIFLE
   Hero's character (Adam Ballard) is developed. His mission: to rescue an uncle who is in trouble.

2. TROUBLE AT THE SILVER SPUR
   Ballard arrives at Three Forks, Texas, where the story is to unfold. He meets the local sheriff and finds out his uncle has been killed. He has his first troublesome encounter with a protagonist and finds his first ally (Monty Flach).

3. DANGEROUS ENEMIES
   Ballard meets John Hayes, owner of the local newspaper, a second ally. He begins to get an idea of what is going on. His room is ransacked and he is hit on the head. Later, he discovers he is being watched and observes a suspicious meeting taking place.

4. SITTING TARGET
   Ballard and Monty ride out to the uncle's ranch, and they are ambushed on the way.

5. BETWEEN A ROCK AND THE THORNS
   Ballard flushes the attacker out. The bad guy gets away, but Ballard discovers the bushwhacker is wearing a boot with a cracked heel.

6. SURPRISE AT THE CIRCLE B
   Ballard and Monty arrive at the Circle B (Ballard's uncle's ranch). They are surprised and disarmed by a friend of the dead uncle. The friend's name is Frank Bridges and he becomes a third ally. Bridges character is developed. Interior of the ranch headquarters is described.

7. RUSTLER'S TRAIL
   While making an initial inventory of livestock, Ballard and Monty discover and follow the trail of three rustlers.

They do not find the rustlers, but they do find a singing woman.

8. THE SINGING WOMAN
    Ballard has first contact with Apache. Meets singing woman (Linda). Linda's character is developed. She is taken to Three Forks. Local residents are introduced. Ballard bumps into second woman (Virginia Murphy). This leads to a fist fight with the foreman of her father's ranch.

9. LIQUID GRACE
    Ballard is formally introduced to Virginia Murphy. She is described. Ballard learns there is a note on the Circle B and it is about to be foreclosed.

10. CRUDE, RUDE, TONGUE-TIED, AND IN LOVE
    Ballard investigates I.O.U. (the note) and finds out it has a thirty-day grace period. Ballard talks to Virginia Murphy again and realizes he may be falling in love with her.

11. THE BULL THROWERS OF CHERRY CREEK CANYON
    Ballard explains his plan for saving the ranch to Bridges and Monty. The plan consists of a roundup, trail drive, and sale of cattle. Roundup begins, and we meet an old moss back longhorn bull that will later play a prominent role in the story.

12. NORTH TO THE CONCHO
    The trail drive starts with the herd headed north toward the Paint Rock on the Concho river.

13. APACHE RAIDERS
    A band of Apache are introduced and described as the first threat to the trail herd.

spectacular that it's almost like a circus. He is paid in gold for the herd.

19. THE BEST-MADE PLANS

Ballard heads back to Three Forks with the gold to save the ranch. His enemies send a crew to steal the gold so the I.O.U. cannot be paid and they will get Ballard's ranch. Ballard realizes he is being followed and hides part of the gold. Ballard is chased, shot, robbed, and left for dead. He survives and Bridges and Monty attend to his wounds. Ballard discovers the robbers did not get the hidden gold and that he still has enough to pay the I.O.U. Ballard embarks on a desperate ride and saves the ranch.

20. BLOOD IN HIS BOOTS

Linda nurses Ballard back to health. He feels obligated to her for saving his life. As Ballard recovers, he finds himself obligated to one woman and in love with another. As Linda connives to marry Ballard, he finds there are factors beyond his control making him more and more obligated to marry her.

21. FRAMED FOR MURDER

Conspirators plan to get rid of Ballard and Virginia Murphy at the same time. Ballard is framed for the murder of Red Murphy(Virginia's father). Ballard is arrested and thrown in jail. Linda and Virginia have a confrontation at Ballard's jail cell. Ballard has a vague feeling of mistrust toward Linda.

22. WHISTLING UP TARGET

Ballard can call his horse with a whistle. He uses this trick to break out of jail but only after almost being hung and fighting a lynch mob. After escaping, Ballard leads a posse into the desert. He losses the posse and returns to the hidden valley to meet Bridges and Monty.

23. BURNING BRIDGES
The Circle B headquarters is burned and in the process
Frank Bridges is captured, beaten, tied up, and left to
burn. He escapes the fire but is severely burned. Bridges
and Monty flee to the hidden valley. They find a cave in
the hidden valley that the outlaws and Indians have been
using for a hideout. They also discover some coal that the
Indians have been using for fuel.

24. BUZZARDS GATHER
Molly O'Brain follows Linda to a meeting of the bad guys.
She overhears the conspirators making plans to destroy
Ballard and Virginia Murphy.

25. A LITTLE OFF CENTER
Ballard and the owner of the local newspaper (Hayes) find
evidence proving Ballard is not guilty.

26. KILLED BY A DEAD MAN
Bridges is confronted at the Circle B and kills one of the
conspirators.

27. THE TEXAS RANGER
Hayes wires the Texas Rangers asking for help.

28. TRAILING THE KILLER
Ballard follows Red Murphy's real murderer. The trail
leads to town where it is lost in the traffic. Ballard goes to
meet Monty and Bridges. He stops at the Circle B where
he finds a fresh grave.

29. THE KIDNAPPING OF VIRGINIA MURPHY
Virginia tries to find Ballard but is kidnapped, abused,
and held prisoner.

30. A SMOKE-FILLED ROOM
The conspirators and their crew head for a confrontation
with Ballard and his men. Molly learns of the meeting

and is at a loss to help because she does not know who to trust with the information.

31. RANGER ON THE TRAIL

A Texas Ranger arrives in Three Forks. Hayes shows him the evidence and convinces the Ranger of Ballard's innocence. Hayes also learns of the railroad plans to come to Three Forks. Hayes meets a man from the railroad. The railroad man explains about the needed right of way on the Circle B and the coal deposits. Molly arrives and tells of the conspirator's plan to kill Ballard and Virginia.

32. THE KIDNAPPER'S NOTE

Ballard finds out Virginia has been kidnapped. Just as he is about to leave on a rescue mission, he receives a note from the kidnappers. Ballard has to follow orders or Virginia will be killed.

33. VIRGINIA STRIKES BACK

Virginia has to fight off an attacker who plans to rape and kill her.

34. A LITTLE INSURANCE

Ballard, Monty, and Bridges get ready for the confrontation with the bad men by hiding weapons and asking the Apache for help. The bad men arrive, the Indians arrive, Ballard and his crew retrieve their arms, and the fight is about to start.

35. THE OPENING OF THE BALL

Ballard and his friends win the fight and most of the conspirators are killed. Ballard reveals there is a "head man" back in Three Forks, and he knows who it is. Ballard goes to Three Forks and shoots it out with "mister big." This chapter ends with Ballard wounded and unconscious.

36. CURTAIN CALL

Mystery is unraveled. Virginia and Ballard plan to marry.

— Chapter One —

The Sixteen-Note Henry Rifle

ANGER WELLED UP IN Adam Ballard, and he was a hard man to rile; but once he was mad, it was just as hard to cool him down. He didn't forgive or forget easy. It was like riding a bucking bronc—sometimes it's harder to get off than it is to ride that old horse to the end.

Anger and meanness didn't run in his family. In fact, for seven generations they'd been known for two main things (not counting having kids, of course, they had lots of kids). First of all for being kind. Kind people, you know the ones you would like to have as neighbors, the ones who bring over cake or chicken when you're ill or when someone dies, not 'cause they're supposed to, but because they have love inside. Adam knew his dad was like that, and he was trying to be as like him as he could.

And second, his family had always been musical. Music and kindness just naturally seem to run hand-in-hand, have you noticed? Well anyway, Adam grew up around fiddles, banjos, mouthharps, flutes, guitars—you name it, and someone in his family could play it. His grandpa died when his dad was nine. So he never knew his grandpa, but oldsters told him they'd danced many a mile to his grandpa's fiddlin' and said they'd ride hours, after a full day's work, just to go to a dance where he was playing.

Others recall how Adam's grandpa would ride by on the wagon playing away on that fiddle. Sure took the sting out of hard work to hear the joy of the music, his long silver hair blowin' in the wind, the music driftin' softly to their ears. Some said they just naturally went to church more often when Adam's grandpa was around. When his grandpa died, Adam's dad and his Uncle Benny took up the family music tradition. Adam's Uncle Benny was his dad Lute's favorite brother, and that means a lot when you have six. His dad played the guitar and Ben fiddled and many a night Adam went to sleep to their playing.

Those who have heard the history of his family often wonder what musical instrument Adam plays. Well, the answer is none. Oh, he probably could have, but he was born different: he was born hungry. From the first time he opened his eyes, he was starved. There was music all around but not much to eat. His family was so busy strummin', fiddlin', and tappin' they didn't have time to grow, trap, or hunt. By the time he was eight, he had figured out if he didn't catch, shoot, or grow it, he wouldn't get anything to eat. By twelve, he was providing most of the food for the family, and he had found the instrument he played best: the sixteen-note Henry rifle (although he played the six-note Navy Colt revolver equally well). In fact, any weapon just naturally seemed to fit his hand—the knife, tomahawk, bow and arrow were all instruments in his band. People said he was a lot like his grandpa, in that when someone had seen him play his instruments, they just naturally went to church more often.

In any event, more than twenty years had passed since he was a boy and now he had another worry. It was a note from his Uncle Ben, and each time he read it, he got madder. The letter reached him at Jackson Hole. It was in his uncle's sprawling hand and simply read, "Come help me, much trouble, watchin' my back, thieves around, be careful," and it was signed, "Uncle Benny." It was postmarked two months earlier in Three Forks, Texas, which Adam later found was north of San Antonio.

Now Adam loved his dad, but he had too much pride to tell him so when he was still alive. But next to his dad, he loved his Uncle Benny and he was still alive, or so he believed, so when Ben called, he went; he didn't ask why, he just saddled up and left. Anyone stealin' from Uncle Benny was going to get a long muddy road and Adam was comin' to deliver it.

— Chapter Two —

Trouble at the Silver Spur

ONE MONTH TO THE day after receiving Uncle Benny's letter, Ballard rode a weary, sore-footed horse into Three Forks. As he walked his horse slowly down the dusty street, heads turned. Old men were sitting in their oak chairs in front of the Silver Spur Saloon spitting, whittling, and swapping stories as they did in all towns; and as he passed headed for the livery, he heard snatches of conversations.

"Nother stranger . . . traveled far, Texas saddle, nice piece of horse flesh, best I've seen lately."

Well, it was true, most people didn't notice Ballard right away, but they always noticed his horse Target. He'd raised Target from a colt. Bought him off an angry horse-raiser in the Indian territory; man was raising Morgan horses and when one of his prize mares was in season, a wild stallion broke in and had his way with her. The rancher thought it was a mustang stallion, but Ballard didn't care at the time and now he knew it just couldn't have been true. Target was too large and well formed to have been sired by a mustang. He stood almost sixteen hands high, and he was solid black except for a derby-sized white spot on his left hip. His head was lean and bony, ears small and very fine, but wide apart. His eyes were medium size, inky dark and prominent, and showed no white round the lid. He was a fast walker and had the lines of speed. His gait was slow and smooth and once he hit it, Ballard could seat himself comfortably, lean against the stirrups, and miles would flow past.

Eventually coming to Lindner's Livery, he tossed the boy a quarter and said, "See he gets a half-bucket of oats, some hay, and a good rubdown. We've come a long way."

The boy nodded and smiled as he admired Target with jealous eyes.

"My name's Adam Ballard," he added, "and I'm lookin' for my uncle, Ben Ballard. Do you know his place?"

The boy replied, "Harry Lindner, pleased to meet ya," as they shook hands. "Your uncle's place is the Circle B, northwest a few miles, but you better talk to Sheriff Bosque before you ride out there."

Something about the way he said it made a chill run down Ballard's spine.

"You'll find his office in the jail just across the street beside Shorty's Barber Shop."

Now Ballard was no outlaw, he didn't know of ever breaking a single law in his life, but lawmen make him nervous. Why? He didn't know, maybe it's the power they had. Anyway, he was a little shaky as he passed Shorty's Barber Shop. Three Fork's jail was a two-cell affair built of local rock. Its glass-paneled door had "Sheriff Ivan Bosque" painted on it. Ballard noted the name was painted much bigger than the title and wondered if the man thought he was more important than the authority of his office.

He knocked and waited for the gruff "Come in" before entering. Next to the door, in the front wall of the jail, was a fly-blown single window, unwashed for years, and it was the only one in this small office. Against the smeared white-washed wall on the left was a rifle rack with two Winchesters and a double-barreled shotgun. On an open shelf beneath the rack were several boxes of cartridges. Hanging nearby, on wooden pegs, were rusty hand and leg chains. Across from him was a paint-flaking iron door leading to the cells in the back.

Directly beside the rack stood an ancient rolltop desk at which a large beefy man sat. He was turned sideways with his back partly toward the front door. Ballard could see a sheriff's star pinned to the brown leather vest he was wearing over a blue checkered shirt. The desk was cluttered with stacks of yellowed newspaper, "wanted" posters, a broken spur, an old pistol, and miscellaneous gear. He appeared to be reading something and didn't rise, extend his hand, or even look up. He just said, "What can I do for you?"

From what Ballard could see, the sheriff's face was shrewd and guarded with weather wrinkles at the outer corner of his eyes. His shoulders were nearly as thick as they were broad, but his head was curiously small. His hands were scarred and his fingers twisted and crooked as if from many fights. He was wearing a black string tie and he was the last man Ballard would have liked to meet in a dark alley.

"Harry Lindner said I should stop by before I rode out to my uncle's place. My name is Adam Ballard and my uncle is Ben Ballard."

He seemed to flinch; he appeared almost startled as he looked up from his papers and studied Ballard with cunning and merciless eyes for several moments. Ballard was a tall 6'2" and weighing 195 pounds. His skin was tanned from the sun. Long arms attached to a broad chest that sloped down to a flat stomach and narrow hips. Green to hazel eyes around a Roman nose, teeth even and white, and rather large lips which turned up on the end making it seem he was always smiling. His short hair was brown to sandy. Finally, Bosque said, "Well I'll be damned, I didn't know Ben had any relatives. Do you have any identification?"

"I've got this," Ballard said, taking his uncle's letter out of his pocket and handing it to the sheriff. Bosque read it carefully several times and eventually said, "Well, 'fraid I got bad news for you. Ben is dead, dead now for almost two months. Died in a gunfight over a card game."

Ballard leaned back against the door jam in stunned silence. Uncle Ben in a gun fight? Never! He made music, not violence; a gentler soul never lived, and hell, he didn't even play cards. It was a family joke he was so bad no one would play with him. Ballard's dad, a fair poker-player, had tried to teach Ben, but he had no head for remembering the cards. Realizing it was hopeless, Uncle Ben had sworn off cards. So Ballard knew something was very wrong here. There just had to be some mistake.

The sheriff went on, "Yeh, he lost $2,000 to Chester Roberts, the local banker, and signed an I.O.U. Later on, he got the idea he'd been cheated and he confronted two of the other players, Ed Seiker and Lanny Weitzel from the Rockin M. They took offense at being called cheaters and when he drew on them, he was killed. There were two other witnesses, Bud Hardin, foreman of the Rockin M, which is the biggest ranch in the area and Paul Horan who owns the local General Store, so no charges were filed."

Ballard stood quietly, studying the lay of the land. He didn't know if the Sheriff was his own man or if he was in someone's pocket. Finally, Ballard picked up the letter, folded it, and returned it to his pocket, saying, "Sheriff, do you know what my uncle could have meant when he mentioned thieves and watching his back?"

"Well, he could have been talking about several things. We've had considerable trouble with Indians stealing horses, cattle, and attacking outlying ranches; in fact, there was a raid on the John Gamble ranch over near Fort Mason last week and fifteen horses were stolen. Your uncle's place is isolated, and maybe it was the Indians he was talking about. At the same time, we've also had trouble with rustlers. They can head almost any direction from here, so this is a popular place for owlhoots. He could have been talking about them. Besides these, your uncle was having trouble with Murphy's Rockin M over land and water rights. He claimed the south side of the North Llano River along with several springs, and Red Murphy, owner of the Rockin M, believes he controls the springs and the whole river."

"Did anyone bother to look at the deed?"

"No one, to my knowledge, has seen a deed. The Rockin M claims that area is public land and they control it by first use. Your uncle said it was deeded land and he had a deed, but no one has ever seen it."

"Couldn't you just check the land office deed records?"

"I did. The page with the date he said he bought the land was missing from the book."

"Didn't the missing page make you suspicious?"

"It sure did and no doubt whoever is lying tore it out, but which one did? I've got to enforce the law impartially, and until I get clear proof, I can't side with either one. Now that your uncle's dead, we'll probably never find out."

"Oh, we'll find out, count on it, because I'm going to get to the bottom of this. In the meantime, the boundaries of his place will remain exactly where he thought they were."

"Well, that's yet to be settled between you and the Rockin M, and I suspect Red will have quite a bit to say on that subject before it's over, but let me make myself clear. If you break the law or even the peace, you better be able to play solitaire."

"Solitaire? Why should I know how to play solitaire?"

"Because you'll need to have something to do while you're here in jail. No stranger is going to come in my town and push local people around, so you better watch your step."

"Sheriff, you've made yourself perfectly clear. Now let me do the same. My uncle was murdered, and he was murdered by local people. Someone is going to pay for his death, local or not, your town or not. Now, you can help me or stand aside and let me do the work, your choice. But once I prove what I'm saying, you better not stand in my way."

With this, Ballard turned and walked out, slamming the door. Standing on the boardwalk, he spotted the Silver Spur and crossed the street. He was dead tired, frustrated, hurt, and angry. As he pushed through the swinging doors and stepped into the gloomy interior, he heard, "If you ride for the brand, you don't say things like that."

Then, "I don't ride for the brand. I'm drawing my pay."

As Ballard's eyes adjusted, he looked down the oak bar and saw a tall wiry puncher with his back to the bar, surrounded by three men like a cat the hounds had cornered. He had a pistol in his hand, but as Ballard watched, one of the men suddenly grabbed the pistol's barrel and violently twisted. The pistol came free and was tossed to the floor. As the pistol fell, the man in front whipped a right to the puncher's jaw and, as he bounced off the bar, a left to his stomach. He fell heavily and attempted to rise, but all three began to systematically kick and stomp him.

Before Ballard realized what he was doing, bile rose in his throat and all the anger of the day rushed to his brain, and suddenly he wanted to hurt, to kill. He snatched a half-full whiskey bottle from the bar, stepped forward, and crashed it on the head of the nearest stomper. The bottle shattered, dropping him like a polled ox. As the man fell, Ballard's hand continued downward, releasing the broken bottleneck and drawing his pistol. Its muzzle was centered on the belt buckle of the larger man before he or the other man could react.

Ballard's voice—so gruff he hardly recognized it—said, "Looks like you boys've kinda stacked the odds in your favor, haven't you?"

"What business is it of yours?" the larger of the two asked. "You'd better take a walk or you'll get some of the same."

Ballard slipped his pistol into its holster and said, "Come on, I'm ready. In fact, I'm more than ready. I just rode in from a long trip. I'm hot and need a drink, and I don't like anything I've seen or heard in this town. So if you want some of me, let's go."

Both men looked surprised; they were evidently accustomed to being known and feared, but in Ballard, they faced an uncertainty, someone not afraid, someone ready to fight.

Suddenly the larger one said, "There'll be another day."

He reached down, picked up his fallen comrade and threw him over his shoulder as if he were a feather, and then they turned and walked around Ballard out the door. The puncher rose on wobbly feet. Ballard held up two fingers to the bartender and said, "Whiskey," followed by, "Looks like you could use a drink."

As the two drinks arrived, the puncher said through busted lips, "Thank you twice, once for my life, or at least for saving me several broken bones, and second for the drink." As he smiled through the pain, Ballard could see he had a good sense of humor and liked him immediately.

The puncher extended his hand and said, "Monty Flach, recently of the Rockin M but presently unemployed." Ballard told him his name and Monty immediately asked if Ballard was related to Ben Ballard.

"He was my uncle."

"I was mighty sorry to hear he was killed. Everyone loved your uncle. He played the fiddle at all the local dances."

"Did you ever see my uncle play poker or carry a gun?"

"No, I never did. In fact, it seems out of character for him."

"What do you know about the night he was killed?"

"Not anything. I was out of town. Me and two other hands were taking a small herd of cattle to Calvert to sell, and it all happened before we got back."

"Have you done ranch work long?"

"Yep, all my life."

"How would you like to work for me?"

"Well, I guess I better, cause soon as local people find out you had trouble with the three men who just left, you'll be about as popular as a skunk under the porch. You'll never get anyone to work for you."

"Who are those guys? Are they that well liked around here?"

"The big one, Bud Hardin, is foreman of the Rockin M. He's known as a tough man and has never lost a fight. He likes violence. Likes to stomp, kick, and beat people near to death. Once he gets his hands on you, he'll not let go until you're crippled. It's not in him just to beat someone—he has to break their spirit.

"The other two, Ed Seiker and Lanny Weitzel, are Hardin's top gun-hands. Weitzel, the one you hit, shot your uncle. Some people call him 'Lanny the Weasel,' but only behind his back and always out of earshot. As you probably saw, he's small, only about five foot five and 135 pounds. He's nervous, herky-jerky, picking things up, touching his hat, his lips, loosening his guns, checking his cartridges, always moving. It's said he's killed nine men and is lightning fast on the draw. Most people avoid him because he has a mean streak and is a killer by nature. If I were you, I'd watch out for him because he'll be out to get even."

Sipping his drink Monty made a face at the sting of the whiskey on his cut lip. As the hurt faded, he continued. "Ed Seiker is kind of an unknown quantity. He's overshadowed by Hardin and Weitzel, but many people think he's the most dangerous of the three. He hardly ever talks, but he's always watching like a hawk. His eyes are piercing and alert, and he's got a hooked beak like a vulture. So, as far as these three being liked, they are not. Local people value their skins too much to cross the Rockin M."

Ballard finished his drink, put a quarter on the bar, and handed Monty two silver dollars. "I'm going to get a room at the Frontier for tonight. Maybe you better too. We'll ride out to the ranch tomorrow. Meet me at first light at the livery."

"You're the boss," Monty said.

Ballard turned and walked out the door and over to the livery where he retrieved his bedroll and saddle bags.

At the two-story, white-painted Frontier hotel, he paid for a night in advance and found his room on the second floor facing the street. Unrolling his bedroll, he took out his razor and a bar of yellow soap. Stripping off his dusty shirt and kerchief, he washed and shaved. When he was finished, he took a clean shirt from his saddlebags and put it on. Afterwards, he thought he might watch the traffic on the street outside, but instead he lay down on the bed and was instantly asleep.

— Chapter Three —

Dangerous Enemies

BALLARD WOKE ABOUT AN hour later, much refreshed, and went down to the dining room. It was late for dinner, and Ballard was alone except for a gentleman reading a newspaper. He was a tall and lean gray-haired man. He wore a dark business suit, shined black half-boots, and a black string tie at the collar of his white linen shirt. As Ballard sat down at the table next to him, he looked up and said, "You must be Adam Ballard, and you're no friend of Bud Hardin and the Rockin M." His eyes twinkled at Ballard's obvious surprise.

"How did you know?"

"It was mostly deductive reasoning. I'm John Hayes, owner of the Three Forks Bugle." He indicated the newspaper with a nod of his head. "I ran into Sheriff Bosque earlier and he mentioned your name. Then as I was coming to dinner, I noticed Bud Hardin and Ed Seiker out front of the Silver Spur helping Lanny Weitzel on his horse, like he'd been in a fight or something. Now you come in, you're a stranger, you resemble Ben Ballard, and no local person would be crazy enough to tie into those three. Any average newspaperman could have reached the same conclusions."

But once he said this, he looked puzzled and went on, "The only thing I don't understand is why you're not thrashed, skinned, shot, cut, or injured in some way."

Ballard explained he had simply gone to the aid of Monty Flach and how the three had decided two wasn't nearly as much fun as one. So since he was never involved in the fight, there were no injuries.

Hayes absorbed this like a dry towel soaks up water and kept nodding as if expecting more. When Ballard made no move to oblige, he said, "You picked the most dangerous men in the area as your enemies. If you want some advice, which is probably worth exactly what I'm going to charge for it, don't ride alone, don't go in dark places, sit with your back to the wall, and don't go anywhere that doesn't have a back door."

The waitress came over and took Ballard's order for the only thing on the menu—steak, potatoes, and coffee—and as she walked away Hayes said, "I think you'll find I have a reputation for being fair and honest and right down the middle of the road, so if you need help, or hear news, please let me know. If it's after business hours, I live in a white house with red-trimmed windows fronting Main Street just past Molly's Boarding House."

With an opening like that, Ballard couldn't resist, "As a matter of fact, Mr. Hayes, you can help. You probably know more about local matters than anyone. What do you know of my uncle's death?"

"Your uncle's death wasn't the first; it was different because it was the first one that occurred in town, but in fact, it seems to be part of some kind of overall plan to run people out of this area." He then rattled off half a dozen names. "One at a time, these people have been singled out, their beef run off, their crops destroyed, out-buildings burned, even their houses."

"What happened to these people?"

"Some were scared and pulled up stakes, some sold for a fraction of what they put in their places, others had convenient accidents and died. Bill Perry had his eldest son bushwhacked and killed. Tom Morrison lost a brother. Perry and Morrison both moved out. This has been going on for over a year and there's others if I can remember 'em."

"Who bought their places?"

"Well, that's the odd part. Most local people think Murphy and the Rockin M are behind the trouble, and it does seem they are always at or near the scene. But to my knowledge, Red has bought only one place and it adjoins his ranch on the north. All the other places were bought by a local lawyer. No one knows and the lawyer won't tell if he's acting for himself or as a front for Murphy or for somebody else."

"Does Sheriff Bosque know what's going on?"

"He knows all right. He'd have to be blind not to, but for some reason he hasn't investigated very much. There's been speculation, but it's hard to say why. He could be in on the deal; on the other hand, it may be as he says. No real complaints have been filed and all the trouble has occurred in the outlying areas, not in town where he has jurisdiction. He's only a town sheriff, but he's the only law in our area. If we had specific information, we could get the State Police out of Austin or the Rangers who have a camp on Honey Creek about fifty miles from here. So far, we've drawn a blank on real evidence. Dead and terrified people tell few tales."

The waitress brought Ballard's food and as he ate they made small talk about the local weather and range conditions and the like. Ballard finished his meal, but now he had more to digest than food.

As Ballard rose to leave, Hayes said, "Are you going to visit your uncle's ranch soon?"

And Ballard replied. "First light in the morning."

"Well, good luck. Maybe nobody's bothered the place. If they have, would you let me know?"

Ballard said he would, they exchanged goodnights, and Ballard headed up to his room. As he unlocked the door, he saw a shadow out of the corner of his eye; but before he could react, the darkness exploded in pain as he was hit a stunning blow on the head. Half conscious, on his hands and knees, he saw a pair of brown leather boots rush past into the hall. Ballard grabbed the door facing and pulled himself up, drawing his pistol, and stepped unsteadily into the hall. Nothing but an open window at the end, with the curtain still moving.

Now, Ballard's mother didn't raise any idiots, and he wasn't going to be the first one by rushing to a lighted window over a dark alley. So he went back into his room, locked the door, and propped the only chair under the door knob. Evidently there was an ample supply of skeleton keys around, but a sturdy chair would stop all but the most determined night crawlers. His saddlebags and bedroll were on the floor with the contents spilled. The mattress on the bed was turned out of place. Picking up his gear and straightening the mattress, he didn't light the kerosene lamp. He wet a wash cloth from the water pitcher at the dry sink and rubbed his face and the back of his neck and head. There was a bump but his hat and thick hair had absorbed much of the force of the blow so the damage wasn't bad. He'd live with nothing worse than a headache.

After he finished his nursing, he moved over to sit on the edge of the bed. The headboard was against the outside wall and when you lay down you faced the door. On the left of the bed was a window with curtains, and that's where Ballard was sitting. It was completely dark outside, and as long as he didn't light the lamp, it was darker in his room than outside so he could see out but no one could see him. Lights were on across the street in several of the shops, but there was a dark alley between the Three Forks Bugle and Horan's General Store; and as he looked, he noticed the burning ember of a cigarette tip glowing. Someone was standing in the alley across from the hotel. They might be watching Ballard's room, at least, they were up to no good, standing in the darkest part of the alley. As he watched, the figure of a man crossed in front of the window of the Three Forks Bugle.

Ballard looked past the newspaper office in the direction from which he had come and saw the Rancher's Bank. The stranger stopped and was talking to whoever was in the alley. Another person came from the other direction, and this time Ballard recognized the burly figure of Sheriff Bosque. He also stopped in the mouth of the alley. Ballard watched for fifteen minutes and finally the first man crossed the street and went into the hotel right under Ballard's window. As he did, Ballard got a good look at him and would remember him when he saw him again. At the same time, Sheriff Bosque walked up past the bank toward the residential part of town and disappeared. The cigarette was gone, but Ballard had the feeling the man was still there.

It had been a long day, with lots of tension and Ballard was exhausted. He took his boots and gun belt off, hanging the belt on the headboard. He made sure the pistol was loose in the holster and its handle was near his hand. Leaving the rest of his clothes on, he eased his sore head carefully down on the pillow, but sleep didn't come right away.

His thoughts were tumbling over each other. Why was his uncle murdered? And by whom? He didn't appear to have had many enemies. So what was the reason? What did he have of value? His ranch? Cattle? After hours of tossing and turning no answers came, and Ballard drifted into a troubled sleep.

— Chapter Four —

Sitting Target

THE REST OF THE night passed without incident, and Ballard's eyes opened in the sullen blackness that precedes dawn. He pulled on his boots, washed his face, picked up his gear, and headed for the livery. On the way he made a detour to the mouth of the alley across the street. Kneeling and striking a match, he could see evidence of a patient man—at least fifteen cigarette butts. He had spent several hours here, and Ballard noticed one other thing—the heel on his left boot was cracked. Well, "At least I know something about him," Ballard thought, as he headed on to the livery.

As he approached the big double doors, Monty stepped out leading their two horses. Seeing him with the horses saddled and ready to go made Ballard feel good, like he had hired the right kind of man.

Mounting, they rode north. The land gradually opened into a huge valley. This valley was the eastern half of the Llano River watershed. The semi-arid land brought to Ballard's mind how tough it was to live here. Everything had stickers, thorns, or a stinger. To exist here you had to be strong. Anyone who roped an old mossbacked longhorn could have told you that with no trouble. The ground was covered with lush grasses that grew mainly in clumps and some were three feet high. Ballard knew this kind of grass was rich in minerals and it made cattle sleek and fat.

As they walked, Target, like a hound on a leash, was eager to get out of control. He strained on the bit, turned his head side-to-side, and rolled his eyes, wanting Ballard to release the reins so he could run.

Target was impatient and decided to play one of his favorite games and pretend to bite Ballard's foot. Ballard knew it was a game but was never completely sure Target did; so, in self-defense when the horse's beaver-like teeth approached Ballard's foot, he reached down and gently pushed Target's head away.

As Ballard leaned over to push, a shot boomed and a slug whistled where Ballard's body had been a moment before. Target got his wish—Ballard's knees hit his sides along with a slap of his hand, and, Indian-like, Ballard leaned over his horse's off side as they broke for the shelter of a thicket.

Another shot boomed and Ballard heard the bullet strike, but it was well off the mark. Ballard and his horse slid to a stop behind the brush and as he dismounted, his Winchester was in his hand. For the last few minutes, they'd been riding along a seasonal creek running down into a large hollow. They were almost at the bottom and Ballard looked back to see Monty behind a bank cut by the creek. He had his Winchester and he was looking up a tree-covered slope. As Ballard watched, a shot kicked dirt over the bank onto Monty's head and immediately Monty rose and returned the fire. Ballard figured there was only one sniper or Monty would've been dead. When there's two, one shoots and the other waits for the counter. If you show yourself, you're dead.

Ballard, hidden from the sniper's view, picked up a rock and threw it near Monty. When Monty looked, Ballard signaled he was going around the thicket to flank the bushwhacker. He also pointed his rifle up the hill and motioned so Monty would know to cover him.

— Chapter Five —

Between a Rock and the Thorns

EASING AROUND THE BRUSH on the left, Ballard came to a gully that had been cut by runoff water into the side of the hill. Actually, it was two hills, with the higher one on the left and the gully cut toward its crown. The sniper was on the lower hill to the right. If Ballard stayed in the bottom of the wash, he would be moving away from the sniper's location but could reach the hill above him without being seen.

As Ballard worked his way up, he continued to hear shots from both Monty and the sniper. Finally, the watershed petered out in a grove of large trees. Ballard snaked on his belly from one trunk to another until he was looking over the lower hill. It was about a hundred yards away, but nothing was moving or looked suspicious. Monty shot and Ballard saw his slug kick dirt near a thick patch of cactus. Ballard looked carefully around that area and noticed about four inches of rifle barrel sticking out on the other side of the prickly pear. The sniper was bellied down on the brow of the hill and on the opposite side of a patch of cactus as tall as a man's head. In addition, there was a large rock just on his other side.

Ballard aimed about thirty inches back from the end of the rifle barrel and began to fire as rapidly as he could crank his Winchester's lever. Six shots through the prickly pear about a foot high and six inches apart and then four more off the rock on the other side. The rifle barrel disappeared, the cactus shook, and a man yelled twice in pain and then viciously cursed. Ballard had to smile, picturing the sniper rolling around between the rock and the thorns, being struck by chips and stickers, and burned by slugs. The next thing Ballard heard was the sound of horse's hooves beating a retreat from behind the hill.

Ballard worked his way over to where the sniper had been. When he got there, Monty was waiting. There were traces of blood on the big rock so Ballard knew he had nicked the sniper, but the small amount indicated he probably hadn't been severely wounded.

Where the sniper had stretched out were several cigarette butts and some empty .41 caliber casings, and just as Ballard had suspected, the clear print of a cracked left boot heel.

— Chapter Six —

Surprise at the Circle B

BALLARD AND MONTY RETURNED to their horses, mounted up, and rode out of the hollow. The range opened up before them in a large basin. They could see the Llano escarpment several miles away to the north and west. At this distance, it looked like a hazy, soft wall, but Ballard knew that up close, it was a sheer rock cliff in many places.

After riding for some time, they came to a fork in the trail. A plank had been nailed to a post with a pointed end on the left and the Circle B brand burned on its surface. Following the path indicated by the sign, they soon began to see scattered cattle, some branded Circle B but mostly Rockin M.

Finally, in the distance they saw some structures in a grove of trees on a small flat-topped hill. The land for some distance around the hill was flat and was clear except for a few scattered oak. Ballard could tell that if you were on the hill, you would be able to see anything that moved for a long distance. As they neared, Ballard noticed the trees were cottonwoods, which normally grow around water. He also saw a large barn, a small shop, a bunk house with cook shack attached, a corral, and the house.

The house was made of native rock and logs, as were the out-buildings and corral. They rode up, dismounted, tied their horses to the corral, and started walking toward the house. It was quiet except for the wind in the cottonwood leaves and a quail calling in the distance, so Ballard had no difficulty hearing the rifle being cocked. His hand darted for his pistol but froze when he heard, "Draw that pistol and this .52 caliber Sharps will make your belt buckle part of your backbone."

They were caught like two tenderfeet in an open place. Ballard cursed himself for being so careless. You'd think a fellow who'd recently been shot at would've been more alert, he thought. As they moved their hands away from their pistols, a man stepped through the front door of the house. His rifle was in his hands and pointed at them. He was older, in his late fifties or early sixties, and was completely bald. The buckskins he wore were threadbare but clean. A long knife was in a fringed sheave on his belt and Ballard could see the handle of a pistol sticking out above his pants. On his feet were moccasins rather than boots. His eyes were clear and green above the rifle sight and the barrel was steady as a rock. Ballard had the feeling he was a dead shot.

"The name's Frank Bridges, and who might you be?" "I'm Adam Ballard and this is Monty Flach and we're here to check on my uncle's place."

Bridges spit tobacco juice and scrutinized Ballard closely, then uncocked and lowered his rifle. "My eyes must be going bad. Now that I look, I see Ben in your nose and the shape of your chin and body. You're a Ballard right enough. Ben and I were friends until he was murdered. He fed and staked me many a time. When I heard he'd been killed, I just naturally moseyed down here to keep an eye on his place. I figured somebody from his family would be along sooner or later."

Turning, he led them into the house. The living room was large and breezy. Its hardwood puncheon floor was covered with a multicolored Indian rug. Bows, lances, and shields were scattered about on the walls. A large fireplace dominated the room. Rocks around the mouth were chipped and smoke-stained, and Ballard could tell many a comfortable evening had been spent sitting by the fire. Homemade chairs with leather and rush seats were against the side walls and under the front window was a church bench with corduroy over goose down pillows.

To the right was a hall door and Ballard supposed that would lead to the bedrooms. Bridges, however, led them to the left through an arched doorway into the kitchen. It was a big pleasant room. One wall was stone, the others were log. Against the stone wall was a massive iron range and beside it the sink with a pump; and across from it was a table and chairs. Ballard and Monty took a chair at the table. Facing them was a door leading out back and tacked on it was a calendar from an Omaha packing house. The place was sparsely furnished and didn't have a woman's touch of curtains and the like but otherwise was neat and clean.

Bridges went to the kindling box by the door and got the materials to start a fire in the stove. As the stove started to heat, Bridges went out back and shortly returned with a handful of fresh eggs and a slab of bacon.

"There's chickens in the barn, fly like quail but they lay eggs, and there's bacon in the spring house from the wild hog I shot the other day." Going out again, he returned with an urn saying, "Sour dough, don't get much chance to make it, not in one place long enough."

Soon he was frying up the eggs and the smell of baking biscuits filled the room. By the time everything was ready, Ballard and Monty were starved from the smell. After they finished the main course, Bridges produced a jar of honey.

"Found a bee tree down in the hollow." They used the honey to finish the remaining two-dozen biscuits. Ballard had never had a more satisfying meal.

"Being a bachelor and living on the frontier for the last fifty years," Bridges said, "I've had to cook for myself or starve. I like to cook and it's no chore to me, and it has made me many a friend. Five years ago, I was cleaned out by Indians, stole my traps, furs, and horses. I joined up with John Chisum on a trail drive to Dodge City, handled the chuck wagon, and cooked for thirty wranglers for five months. After we got back, they begged me to stay, said they'd never find a cook as good, but I drew my pay and went back to what I loved best—trapping. Now, five years later, there's not much demand for fur, not much fur around, and I'm getting old so maybe I'll go back to cooking."

Ballard wasn't about to let an opportunity like this slip by, especially with Monty kicking him under the table, so he said, "We'd be proud if you'd stay and help get Uncle Ben's place back on its feet. I don't have a lot of cash, but I can offer your a dollar a day plus found."

Bridges stuck out his hand and they shook, and he said, "Ben would have wanted me to help and I wouldn't be much of a friend if I didn't return the many favors he did me. Will this ranch be yours?"

"Well, Uncle Ben was the last of my uncles and he never married. I've got lots of cousins scattered about, but I was always his favorite. He and my dad did everything together. They were the youngest and I guess it made them closer. They were going to start a ranch together, but while Dad was working on the railroad to raise his share of the money, he was killed in an accident. After that, Ben drifted off and I didn't hear from him again until I got his last letter. I don't know if he had a lawyer or a will, but until I find different, I have the best claim. So I'm going to assume this place is mine till someone proves me wrong and try to fix it up. Tomorrow we're going to start by taking a look around to see what kind of livestock is left."

— Chapter Seven —

Rustler's Trail

THE NEXT MORNING THEY were up at first light and after breakfast, Ballard and Monty struck out to round up whatever Circle B horses they could find. Bridges had a donkey in the barn but did not have a horse, so he was assigned to get the wagon out and grease its hubs, inventory the supplies, and make a list of things needed. Bridges said he had seen a small herd of horses to the northeast, and that's the way Ballard and Monty headed.

By mid-morning, they had located and rounded up fifteen horses and brought them back in. Once they were corralled, Ballard and Monty headed back to look for cattle, and it was then they discovered some puzzling signs. Three men had built a small fire and roped and branded several calves. The calves were still standing nearby bawling their displeasure to their mamas. The problem was each of these calves was following a cow with a Circle B brand, but the calves were branded Rockin M.

Monty indicated the fire was clearly on Circle B range and so Ballard was curious to see who was swinging such a wide loop. Ballard and Monty followed the trail west, and as they went, Ballard wondered what kind of men would rustle his cattle? Were they working for Murphy? It seemed they must be, since they used his brand. Had Murphy ordered them to do it, or were they on their own and trying to stir up trouble? If they were trying to start trouble, why? And why had they been so obvious about the whole thing—the fire and the fresh brands were clear signs to any westerner.

For the first few miles, the riders had made little effort to hide their tracks, or so it seemed. Now, the trail disappeared. Almost as if they had just stepped up into heaven and something told Ballard that wasn't the direction they were eventually headed, especially if he caught them. For the last half hour, the trail had been gradually moving upward out of the bottom until now it was on the crown of a ridge. Rocks were scattered around, some with bright yellow spots on their surface, one resembling a standing jack rabbit. On the left was a limestone bluff of about fifty feet straight up. Its length stretched for miles, marking the edge of the escarpment. At many points, it was possible to walk a horse up the face of the bluff or even occasionally to ride to the top, but this wasn't one of those places. In fact, a monkey would have had trouble going up where the trail ended, so Ballard discarded that option.

To the right, the land sloped down to the bottom Ballard and Monty had come out of, and the ground was soft in many spots so it would have been impossible to go that way and not leave a trail. Nevertheless, Ballard made a circle down the slope hoping to pick up a trace, but he was soon back at the beginning with no sign. Directly ahead, a narrow canyon pointed West to the badlands, an unlikely possibility because Monty said there was nothing in that direction but dry land and Apache, but it seemed to be the only possibility so that's the way they went.

Monty had never been in this particular canyon. It was just on the edge of the Circle B and was known to have little grass of grazing value. As they rode, the walls closed in around them.

Ballard had an uneasy feeling someone was watching them, and he had a sense about such things, but other than the tracks they were making and those of a lone wolf and a few deer, there were no other signs about.

Eventually, the walls opened out into a little valley, no more than forty acres, and where they rode in, there was an old wall around a spring of clear blue water. Ballard could smell smoke and looking across a small stream, he saw several deer. Riding to the top of a small knoll, they were surprised to see what appeared to be a rock cabin against the opposite canyon wall. Smoke was rising from it, and suddenly they heard singing. It was a woman's voice.

— Chapter Eight —

The Singing Woman

JUST THEN THE HORSES' ears went up and Ballard saw the Indians, two Apache belly-down on a knoll near the stream. The Indians had not heard Ballard and Monty approaching because the running water had covered the sound. The Apaches' attention was on whoever was doing the singing. The breeze was in Ballard's face, and the hair on his neck stood up because he could smell them now, a smell not unlike a skunk, sort of a musky, smoky, wild smell. It wasn't entirely unpleasant. It came from the things they ate, their outdoor life, and the grease they rubbed on their bodies to keep the bugs off. But it was a smell once you smelled it, you would never forget; day or night you'd remember.

The horses smelled it too and started to move nervously, but Ballard grabbed his horse's nose and Monty did likewise to keep them from snorting and alerting the Indians. The Apaches were only about fifty feet away, and suddenly the nearest one rose to his knee and drew an arrow from his quiver. Motioning to Monty to take the one on the left, Ballard kicked his horse, drew his Colt, and with a blood curdling scream rode down the Indian on the right. Ballard's horse hit the Apache a spinning blow and then Ballard was over the small knoll. Wheeling Target around on his heels he spurred back in time to see the Indian, minus his bow, disappear into a small grove of cedar directly ahead. Off to Ballard's left, he heard two pistol shots and one from a rifle, but he didn't have time to check them out. He rode to the point where the Indian had disappeared, leaped from his horse, and followed on foot.

The trees were gnarled and twisted, with greasewood bushes underneath. Cedar needles and dead limbs littered the ground. He moved cautiously along a small game trail. There was no sign of the Indian's passage until Ballard spotted a smudge on the moss. As he bent for a closer look, a heavy weight fell onto his back; he didn't resist but let momentum hurl him and the attacker to the ground. They hit with a jarring thud, which knocked Ballard's pistol from his grasp. As the pistol fell, Ballard immediately twisted and pushed up with both arms, throwing the Apache into the brush. Quick as a cat, the Indian was back, his knife going for Ballard's stomach. Knocking the thrust aside, Ballard grabbed the Apache's wrist in his left hand and staggered the Indian with a right to the side of the head. The Apache was a smaller man but had the strength of a wild animal.

Again, Ballard struck, this time to the Apache's throat and again to the head, but the Indian kicked Ballard on the instep and he fell hard. Immediately, the Apache tried to jump on top of Ballard, but as he came, Ballard put his feet onto the Apache's chest and kicked the Indian over his head. The ground shook as he hit and his knife fell at Ballard's feet. Ballard picked up the knife and scrambled to his feet, but snarling deep in his throat, the Apache snatched a tree limb from the ground and struck the white man a savage blow on the side of the neck. The knife flew from Ballard's hand and his shoulder was numb. Ballard was gasping for air and he knew this fight had to end very soon, if it were to end in his favor. The Apache attempted another blow with the tree limb, but Ballard ducked under the swing and picked the Apache up and threw him against a large oak tree. Ballard heard an ugly snap when the Apache hit and saw his right leg give when he tried to rise. Hate was still in the Indian's eyes, but suddenly, they glazed over and he fell unconscious to the ground. Picking up the Apache's knife, Ballard cut some leather fringe from the Indian's buckskins and tied his hands and feet. The Apache groaned when Ballard moved his feet together but otherwise gave no sign of life.

Securing the knots, Ballard retraced his steps out of the grove. As he emerged, he saw Monty, without his hat, pistol in hand, standing over the body of a dead Indian. Monty holstered his pistol and reached down and picked up his hat as Ballard approached. It had a bullet hole near the crown. Sticking his finger through the hole, Monty said, "Lucky for me, he shot a little high or I'd be the one lying here. Where's the other Indian?"

"I tied him up back in the grove. He's alive but his leg is broke."

At this point, a rather flushed whirlwind of blonde hair, curls, and blue dress arrived on the scene.

"I heard shots," she said and then saw the dead Indian and her hand flew up to her throat in fright.

"I didn't know there were Indians in the area," she said.

"Not only are they in the area, but they were about to attack you when we rode up," Ballard replied.

Her face turned pale as she asked, "You said they, where are the others?"

"Actually, ma'am there were only two and the other lies back in the woods with a broken leg."

"How do you know they were going to attack me?"

"When we heard you singing and rode over here, one of the Apache had drawn an arrow and was pointing it in your direction."

Realizing the danger she had been in she stammered, "I guess you think I'm pretty stupid being out here in the wilderness singing my head off. Almost getting myself killed."

As she spoke Ballard took his first good look at her. She was about 5'7" (tall for a woman), had blonde hair, with freckles on her arms and face. She was wearing a simple dress that fell to a well-turned ankle, her eyes were robin's egg blue, her nose smallish, and her lips slightly puckered. Her well-curved chest rose above a small waist, she appeared to be rather long of leg, and was apparently in her early twenties. All-in-all, she was a beautiful woman.

Suddenly, as if a dam had burst, she rushed into Ballard's arms and began to cry like a broken-hearted child. Great sobs came from her throat and tears coursed down her face. Not having been around many women, he didn't know what to do, so he just held her. In a few minutes, the storm was over and she drew back.

"Please forgive me, but I'm all alone here. My dad was with me until yesterday, but he was sick and he died. We only recently left the East and I know nothing of the West, or its customs, or how to provide for myself, and I have no friends or relatives. I'm completely lost and don't know what to do. Yesterday, three men rode up and I thought they might help, but they acted nervous and kept looking back up their trail, as if they were expecting something they were afraid of. Finally, they left, and after they were gone, I discovered our strongbox with $200, all the money we had in the world, was gone. So, here I am a thousand miles from home with no money and no place to go."

Ballard stood for a moment digesting all she had said, and a burning anger grew in the pit of his stomach because he felt the three men who stole her money were also the ones who stole his cattle.

"Don't worry ma'am," he began, but she waved her hand to interrupt him.

"My name is Linda Harrison. Please call me Linda. 'Ma'am' makes me feel so old."

"O.K., Linda, we're not about to leave you here. We'll take you into Three Forks."

With this, her face brightened and a small smile touched her lips.

She said, "Well then, the least I can do is offer you a cup of coffee before we leave. It's one of the only things I still have to share."

"Before we drink coffee, Monty and I had better check on our other Indian friend."

She turned in the direction of the cabin, and Ballard and Monty returned to where Ballard had left the Indian. When they got to the spot, the Apache was gone. Looking around they found the leather bindings on the ground. Ballard could see where the Apache rose and limped out of the grove of trees onto the rock under the canyon wall. Once he was on the rocky shelf, all signs disappeared. There were some bushes against the wall off to the right, but otherwise not a thing in sight. Realizing it was hopeless to try to find him, they turned back.

When they reached the camp, Linda had coffee boiling. They told her the Indian was gone and she didn't seem surprised. As Ballard sipped his coffee, he looked at the stone structure. It really wasn't a cabin but an old wall which formed a wind break. It was about eight feet long and about four feet from the canyon wall facing north. The flat rocks were stacked to a height of about six feet. Anyone building a fire between it and the canyon wall would get a good heat reflection from both directions. Ballard wondered who could have built it. There was no mortar between the rocks, so obviously it hadn't been built in modern times.

As they drank coffee, Linda recounted how she and her father had left the East to head for a dryer climate because he had been ill from consumption. Eventually, they had arrived at San Antonio by stage and had purchased two mules, a wagon, and supplies. Local residents had told them there was plenty of land available in Texas, if they could avoid the Indians.

Six days ago they had left San Antonio traveling in a southeasterly direction but had not liked the looks of the dry lands and had turned north. Her dad's condition had worsened until by the time they got here, he was running a high fever and was delirious. She nursed him as best she could, but he died in his sleep the night before last. The three men had helped her bury him, and she felt they had discovered the strong box while getting the tools out of the wagon.

After coffee, they sand-washed the utensils, hitched up Linda's mules, and headed for town. They reached Three Forks about 4 o'clock in the afternoon. Ballard had tied his horse behind the wagon and was riding on the seat beside Linda. Monty acted as their outrider, and as they passed Lindner's Blacksmith & Livery, Horan's General Merchandise, the Frontier Hotel, The Silver Spur, Western Union Telegraph & Stage, Rancher's Bank, and pulled up at Molly O'Brain's Board and Lodging House, people turned to look and talk.

Molly met them at the front gate. She was a large, big boned woman about fifty years old, handsome but not pretty. Her hair was light red, eyes green, and she stood over six feet tall. She must have weighed close to 200 pounds, but the largest thing about her was evidently her heart. Once Ballard introduced himself and told her Linda's story, she took the girl's hand and said, "Well, you've come to the right place." With this, she pulled Linda into the house, fussing over her like an old hen over little chickens, and said, in parting, "Adam Ballard, you and Monty Flach can come back anytime after she's had a day or two of rest. Until then, we'll not be receiving company."

As Ballard and Monty turned to take the horses and wagon over to the livery, a townsman who seemed vaguely familiar to Ballard walked up. Monty introduced him as Chester Roberts, the local banker. He was a tall, glad-handed, large man, his hair neatly oiled, and he smelled good. His squinty brown eyes were over a pencil mustache and there was something about him Ballard didn't like. Perhaps it was his slick look—maybe too slick.

After they were introduced, Roberts said, "Well, Ballard, what have we here? Who was that woman?"

The question sort of rankled Ballard because he was by nature not very talkative. "Nothing of importance," he replied.

Roberts studied Ballard for a moment and said, "You're a stranger and you come into town with a beautiful woman, she's alone, it's the most exciting thing that's happened in Three Forks in months, and it's nothing of importance?" Ballard was tired, needed a bath, and was maybe a little jealous of Roberts' interest in Linda, so he said, "Why not ask the lady, if you want to know so bad?" and he spun on his heel and left Roberts standing.

As they walked away, Ballard asked Monty, "Is that guy a native Texan?" disbelief in his voice.

"I don't think so, although I don't know him that well. He's only been around town for the last year. After our other banker was killed in an accident, he showed up and bought the bank from his estate and I heard he was from the East."

They looked at each other and smiled as if Ballard's suspicions had been verified. With that, Ballard dispatched Monty to the livery with the horses, and as he did so, he noticed his shirt and jeans were torn from the Indian fight. He headed for Horan's General Merchandise and on the way it came to him why Roberts looked familiar. Roberts was one of the men who had met in the alley, the one who had crossed the street under Ballard's window. Curious, very curious.

As Ballard stepped inside the general store, he spotted a man of possibly forty, his eyes the palest amber under fiercely bushed dark eyebrows. His chestnut hair, short and partless, burred out above a patient face. This almost benign expression was somehow belied by the arrogance in his eyes. He was dressed in a brown suit with a white shirt and string tie and was a round-bodied man, thick at the waist and thicker at the chest. His white fleshy hands had never known a rope burn or hard physical work. On his feet were congress gaiters rather than boots.

As Ballard approached he said, "Mr. Horan?" and as Horan nodded, "I'm Adam Ballard, Ben's nephew. Did my uncle have a credit account here for the Circle B?"

"He sure did, but it didn't have a balance when he died. Why do you ask?"

"I need to use it until we get the Circle B back on its feet."

Horan didn't reply, just reached under the counter and pulled out a receipt book saying, "Sign this and tell me what you need."

Ballard signed and told Horan he needed a fresh shirt, jeans, underwear, and socks. Horan quietly and efficiently gathered these items and wrote the amounts on the receipt. After he finished, he totaled the purchase and handed Ballard a copy of the receipt, placing the original in a little metal box under the counter.

Adam picked up his purchases and his next stop was Shorty's Barber and Bath. He had a trim and shave while Shorty heated a large quantity of bath water. Afterwards, Ballard took a bath to soak most of the trail from his body. Then pulling on his new clothes, he decided to go to the Silver Spur for a drink before dinner. Several horses were tied outside, most with the Rockin M brand. Crossing the street he had to go around a passing wagon and didn't see the young lady carrying several packages until he bumped into her. Packages flew and she lost her balance and fell into a mud puddle.

As she fell, she shrieked, "Oh no, not my new dress!" Ballard reached to help her up and apologize, but a rough hand grabbed his shoulder and shoved him aside. Ballard staggered back off balance until he struck the end of the hitching rail and bounced off to fall to one knee. As he did, a large red-haired, red-faced man brushed past him to help the woman up.

"Are you hurt, sweetheart? Oh, look at your muddy dress."

"No, Dad, I'm not hurt, and the dress will wash." After assuring himself she was all right, the man turned back to Ballard, and almost growled. "Red Murphy's the name and who might you be?"

Before Ballard could answer, three other men stepped off the boardwalk. One was Bud Hardin who said, with a sneer, "This here is Adam Ballard, the gent who blind-sided Lanny at the Silver Spur."

As Hardin spoke, Ballard looked closely at him for the first time. Bud Hardin was about six foot three and weighed close to 230 pounds. He had long arms and large hands. His little pig eyes were squeezed in to either side of a flat nose. His ears were small and close to his head and his hair was thick and wiry.

On his right was Lanny Weitzel, his sharp foxlike face nervous, both hands opening and closing above the two pistols he wore tied down low on either hip.

On his left was Ed Seiker and another man he didn't know at the time but later found out was Plunk Murray. Seiker's hooded eyes were watchful and alert.

Plunk Murray was the odd one of the lot, a real cowman by reputation, a westerner. As a nine-year old, after his parents were killed by Indians, he was taken in by Red Murphy. Since then, the Rockin M had been his life. He was now in his late forties and looked like a weathered piece of leather. A thousand lines, wrinkles, and crow's feet were on his sun-browned face.

His hands were calloused from hard work and he was tough as Indian jerky. He was also fair and honest, but in every sense of the word, he rode for the Rockin M.

Bud Hardin had a bright gleam in his eyes as he said, "it looks like this clumsy backwoods yokel needs a lesson in manners. Anyone who would purposely bump into a pretty girl deserves a beating."

Embarrassed by this accusation, Ballard said, "She was carrying packages so she didn't see me, or I her."

"So, she bumped you. She's clumsy, huh?" Hardin asked with a smirk.

With a sudden roar of glee, Hardin sprang, counting on the element of surprise to pin Ballard against the hitching rail. But instead of rising from his knee, Ballard ducked under the rail and Hardin hit it a shattering blow with his stomach and cracked it into three pieces.

The wind left Hardin for a moment and Ballard rose and faced him, saying, "I don't want to fight you, Hardin."

Hardin's only reply was to reach across the shattered rail and backhand him. The force of the blow knocked Ballard down between the rail and the boardwalk. Hardin immediately leaped through the gap trying to stomp him. Before he could, Ballard rolled back under the broken rail to the street and jumped to his feet.

As Ballard rose, someone shoved him and he staggered toward Hardin in time to catch a looping right to the forehead. The sky exploded and Ballard's knees sagged, but he stepped back out of reach with the rail still between them. Ballard heard Monty say, "The next person who shoves is going to eat buckshot." Monty was standing in the Saloon door with the double-barreled shotgun from the bar, and although it wasn't pointing at anyone in particular, it was clear he could bring it to bear and fire before anyone in the street could draw or get out of the way.

Ballard's head hurt, but otherwise he felt confident. He didn't want this fight, but if they were going to push it, someone would pay the price.

Ballard looked at Murphy and said, "You better stop this before someone gets hurt."

Hardin interrupted, "Boss, he's afraid. He wrongs your daughter and he wants you to save his bacon."

Angry, Ballard said, "At least I'm not a cattle thief like some people at the Rockin M."

A knowing look came into Hardin's eyes. Plunk Murray looked puzzled. Murphy, stung by the public accusation said, "Hardin, he's all yours."

A savage look came over Hardin's face, and he came around the rail on the run, his arms spread, intending to wrap Ballard in his massive embrace. Ballard stood his ground and as the big man reached him, turned his body, raising his bent elbow shoulder high, and swinging it to meet Hardin. It caught him in the mouth and the combined force of the swing and his momentum stopped him dead. Ballard stepped to the side and hit him then, a right to the stomach and a left which split his ear. Again, Ballard tried a right, but this time Hardin was ready and grabbed Ballard's arm. Once, twice, three times Ballard hit him with left hooks to the face, but he might was well have been hitting a wall. Hardin reeled him in like a fish, hand-over-hand. Hardin's huge arms locked around Ballard's arms and chest and began squeezing the life slowly out of him. Lifting his feet off the ground, Ballard started to rock back and forth, throwing his weight first in one direction, then in the other. Just as he was beginning to see black closing in, both feet hit the ground at once and he immediately ducked his head and shoved, butting Hardin under the chin and knocking his arms loose. As Hardin's grip loosened, Ballard uppercut a right to his chin. Hardin's head snapped back and he lost his balance and fell.

Hardin rose slowly, shaking his head and Ballard went with a hook to the face and another to the stomach. He was beginning to get his second wind and he stepped in striking to the head, to the throat, and back to the head.

Hardin's ear was torn and hanging, his mouth bleeding, he was breathing hard and as they circled, he said, "Stand still and take your medicine, woman-fighter." Hardin lunged for him at the same instant Ballard stepped for him and they met with a jarring impact. Standing toe-to-toe, they started to slug. A savage joy boiled in Adam Ballard's mind, a maniac lust to smash this man. Ben had been murdered and here was someone to hit.

Ballard saw a looping right coming and ducked, taking it on top of his head. Hardin, shaking his hand, stepped back and Ballard charged, lowering his head and butting Hardin in the chest, knocking him across the boardwalk into the wall of the Silver Spur. As Ballard sprang to follow, Hardin bounced off the wall and delivered a smashing blow, knocking him to the ground. Head down, gasping for breath, Ballard was on his hands and knees when he felt a savage kick in the side. The force of it rolled him under the rail into the street. As he turned, Hardin was standing with his feet wide apart; his face was smeared with blood and agonized with his effort to get his breath. Hardin staggered toward him and Ballard came up driving into him with his shoulder, wrapping his arms around him and lifting.

Hardin clawed at Ballard's back off balance and then his feet lifted and they fell on the boardwalk, splintering one of the boards and driving the back of Hardin's head into the building wall. The fall broke Ballard's grip and Hardin heaved him off, rolling under the rail and rising in the street on the other side. Ballard's chest heaved and he knew the rest had to be brief and vicious, because if he failed in this last burst, he was done.

Wholly demented, Ballard stepped in and threw a flurry of blows, but Hardin absorbed this storm and suddenly kicked Ballard on the knee, tripping him to the street. Instantly, Hardin leaped on top, his big hands tightening around Ballard's throat. Ballard had only moments before Hardin would crush his larynx. As they rolled back and forth, Ballard's hip bumped something and his right hand desperately felt and picked up a broken chunk of the tie rail. He smashed it with all his remaining strength against Hardin head, once, twice, and finally Hardin fell away. Ballard rolled with him and as Hardin came to one knee, Ballard hit him in the mouth. Hardin fell again and on hands and knees spit a broken tooth on the ground. It was clear he'd had enough.

Ballard slumped to sit on the edge of the plank walk, stupid with exhaustion. It hurt to breathe. He sat for a long minute with his head hung between his knees before Monty pulled him to his feet. He rose, weaving drunkenly, and Monty steadied him against the wall as he continued to breathe in great gusts of precious air. After a while, his breathing eased and he raised his head as Murphy and his crew loaded Hardin into a spring wagon.

Murphy said, "You've won this time, but there will be other days. No one calls me a thief, insults my daughter, and attacks one of my men and gets away with it."

Murphy's threat was clear, but Ballard was too headstrong to let anyone tell him what to do, so he just turned and walked into the saloon, saying over his shoulder, "I'll be around whenever you're ready, Murphy."

As soon as they were out of sight, Ballard's pride left him and he said, "Monty, help me to my room."

It seemed unnaturally quiet in the hotel room after the brawling noise of the street fight. After Monty left, Ballard washed the blood from his face. The mirror over the washstand showed him a lip that was split and swollen where it had been mashed against his teeth. He hadn't lost any teeth, but his cheekbone was cut, and so was one of his eyebrows. His right ear was still bleeding and his new shirt hung in tatters. Through its holes, he could see his chest was covered with welts and livid bruises. All his ribs were tender, but feeling each in turn, he didn't think any were broken. Raising his hands to eye level, he looked at his raw and bloody knuckles, and again, although his fingers, hands, wrists, elbows, and shoulders ached painfully, none appeared to be broken. After this last inspection, he was exhausted, fell on the bed, and went immediately to sleep.

— Chapter Nine —

Liquid Grace

AFTER SPENDING THE NIGHT at the Frontier, Monty and Ballard left early the next morning and reached the ranch by midmorning. Bridges had the wagon all greased up, the harness soaped, and a supply list ready, so Ballard decided to immediately return to Three Forks. At the corral, Ballard roped the two horses he suspected of being draft horses, and luck was on his side because they turned out to be harness broke. When they were harnessed up, Ballard stepped into the wagon seat, and telling Monty and Bridges to take some of the rough edges off the remuda, headed back for town.

The trip was uneventful, and when he reached town it was approaching dusk. By the time he loaded up and returned to the Circle B, it would be midnight, and the trail wasn't familiar, so he decided to stay the night at the Frontier again.

He dropped the wagon at Lindner's, checked into the hotel, washed up, and went down to the dining room. In no particular hurry, he lingered as the tables gradually filled up until he was the only person seated alone. His chair was against the wall near the door so he noticed Virginia Murphy as soon as she walked in. Now that he had an opportunity to look at her closer, he realized she was not overly tall, five foot five or so, but she was so well-proportioned she gave the appearance of height. There was something animal about her, almost feline. She moved with a liquid grace. Her eyes were large and when she blinked her long lashes moved almost sleepily. There was a sullen, sultry, dark loveliness about her that made him swallow involuntarily. As she stood in the doorway, her eyes flitted around the crowded room and finally came to him.

He quickly scrambled out of his chair and said, "Won't you please join me?"

She said, "I don't believe we've been introduced. What will people say?"

Well, that's easy to fix. My name is Adam Ballard."

"And I'm Virginia Murphy."

"As far as what people would say, it depends on how hungry you are as to how much you care."

She laughed and said, "You are absolutely right and I'm starved. I never eat breakfast and I was so busy shopping and talking I forgot to eat lunch, so you're stuck with me." There was an attractive twinkle in her eye.

Ballard held her chair for her and once they were seated she said, "Dad says you're related to Ben Ballard."

"He was my uncle."

"I was very sorry to hear of his death. We all miss him so. He was one of the bright spots around here."

"It was my understanding one of your hands shot Ben and that he and the Rockin M didn't see eye-to-eye, especially on land boundaries and water rights."

She blushed but said, "That is true, Mr. Ballard, but your uncle was still cherished by all of us who loved music, no matter what disagreements he might have had with my father or with the crew, and it was my understanding he called Lanny Weitzel a cheater and forced him to draw over a card game. In addition, my father's friends and my friends are not always the same, and his enemies are not necessarily mine. Oh, don't get me wrong, I love my dad and I'm immensely proud of him, and loyal, but I also have a life of my own to live."

Ballard could see a proud and headstrong streak in her and knew she would be a handful for any man.

"After the fight yesterday, Dad was fit to be tied. Not only was his foreman whipped in public, but he also heard Bud Hardin mention he had a scrap with a stranger in town. That wouldn't have been you, would it?"

"I'm afraid it was."

"Dad suspected as much and was very angry because his crew had been backed down in public. He thinks if the Rockin M shows the slightest weakness, people will began to take advantage. Sort of like the lion that falls in front of the hounds—they all rush in for a bite. You don't look like a troublemaker. Are you?"

"I never look for trouble nor do I run if it comes looking for me. I obey the law and try to live my life in an honorable, peaceful manner, but circumstances sometimes prevent it."

"Bud Hardin said you walked up behind Lanny Weitzel and hit him with a whiskey bottle, he didn't know you, hadn't spoken to you, and you didn't even warn him. Is that right?"

Ballard's face turned red in embarrassment. "Some would see it that way, but maybe you ought to check around before you jump to any conclusions."

Her eyes weren't unfriendly, but she had a puzzled look as if there was something she was trying to understand but couldn't quite grasp. She started to speak again, but John Hayes stepped through the door motioning at Ballard. Ballard excused himself, paid for his meal, and walked out on the boardwalk.

"I'm sorry to disturb your dinner," Hayes said, "but I couldn't talk in there and especially in front of Virginia Murphy. I've heard Chester Roberts has a court order and the Sheriff is going to post the Circle B for foreclosure."

— Chapter Ten —

Crude, Rude, Tongue-Tied, and in Love

NEXT MORNING BALLARD WAS at the bank when Chester Roberts arrived.

"What's this about the Sheriff posting the Circle B for foreclosure?" Ballard asked him.

"Your uncle owed me $2,000. I have his I.O.U. The money is owed, he's dead, and I'm not about to let it slip away from me. If you're his heir, then you pay me in cash, and I'll drop the foreclosure."

"I don't have that kind of money and don't know where I could raise it. You'll have to give me time."

"No I don't. The law says thirty days after you're posted. If you don't come up with the money, the ranch is mine. I, like many other people, have financial obligations to meet, I don't know you, don't know if you're a rancher or not, so I have no reason to give you time. For all I know you would just use it to run up more debt and make my I.O.U. worthless. The ranch is due to be posted the first Tuesday of the month, which is tomorrow. You will have thirty days from then to get the money."

There was no use arguing. Ballard could see Roberts' mind was made up, but as he rose to leave he asked, "Could I see my uncle's I.O.U? You say you have it."

A brief shadow crossed Roberts' face and he hesitated, but said, "Of course," and rose and left the room.

He returned shortly with a small strongbox and with a keychain from his pocket he opened it and handed Ballard a small piece of paper. It looked like a regular receipt but simply said, "I.O.U. $2000." and was signed Ben Ballard. Something about the receipt bothered Ballard, something in the back of his mind, but he couldn't recall it. The writing wasn't his uncle's, but it was his signature. It looked legitimate enough, but Ballard knew his uncle didn't play poker. In any event, there was nothing more Ballard could do here at this time, so he handed it back and rose and left the bank.

Ballard went to the livery, hitched up the horses, paid the bill, and pulled over in front of Horan's General Store. Paul Horan was in the store alone and Ballard said, "Good morning," and handed him Bridges' list. As Horan started to accumulate the items, Ballard picked up four boxes of .41 caliber, two boxes of .52 caliber, and six boxes of .45 caliber cartridges and Horan said, "Expecting trouble?"

"No, just believe in being prepared."

He started to carry the provisions out, and by the time Horan had rounded everything up, most of it was loaded. They finished the loading, Horan totaled the amount on Ballard's signed receipt, and handed him a carbon copy, which he put in his back pocket. As he mounted the wagon to leave, Virginia Murphy emerged from the hotel and daintily walked across the street. He got down and took his hat off and laid it on the wagon seat.

"Good morning, Miss Murphy."

She looked stunning and just watching her approach, he felt short of breath.

"Mr. Ballard, we didn't finish our conversation last night, you left in such a hurry. Some of the things you said troubled me, and I tossed and turned last night trying to make sense of them. Perhaps if you have time later, we can finish the conversation."

She was standing quite close and suddenly the nearest horse moved to escape the bite of a horsefly and bumped Ballard. He staggered a step forward, knocking her back. She started to fall and instinctively he snatched her into his arms. Her softness overwhelmed him. Her hair brushed his face and the sweetness of her smell filled his nose.

Ballard's dream was interrupted by, "Mr. Ballard, you can release me now."

When Ballard snapped out of his daze, he was standing there holding her and she was looking right in his eyes. He jumped back against the wagon with a bang, dropping her like a hot coal. He blushed beet red to the roots of his hair and to cover his embarrassment quickly climbed back to the wagon seat and promptly sat on his hat. His red began to turn to purple. He didn't know much about women, but he knew she wasn't the kind you could go around hugging on the main street in broad daylight.

As Ballard untied the reins from the foot brake handle and started to leave, she said, "Mr. Ballard, you never answered my question. Can we finish our conversation later or not?"

Cramming his crushed hat on his head, he got up enough nerve to look down into her eyes and noticed a small smile on her lips. She actually seemed to be enjoying his fit of confusion and discomfort.

"Miss Murphy, nothing in this world would give me more pleasure than talking to you again."

With this, he slapped the horses with the reins and they moved slowly away. As the wagon turned the corner, he glanced back and she was still standing there looking in his direction.

On the long ride back, Ballard kicked himself again and again for acting like a schoolboy. Crude, rude, tongue tied, staggering around like a drunk Indian. His self-image got smaller and smaller the more he thought about it. Why me? Why did she want to talk to me? Was she just curious about why I was so clumsy? Did she think I was touched? Maybe it was her month for charity. Maybe red was her favorite color. Why associate with me? Her father wouldn't like it. Maybe she was just being friendly and had no interest in me otherwise. He felt his heart and spirits plunge at the thought.

Before he noticed it, he was driving into the ranch yard. As he jumped down and started to unload the supplies, he realized he had resolved nothing and the answers would only come with time.

— Chapter Eleven —

The Bull Throwers of Cherry Creek Canyon

AFTER THE EVENING MEAL, Ballard, Bridges, and Monty gathered around the kitchen table and Ballard explained the problem of the I.O.U. and the time deadline.

"My plan," he said, "is to round up the Circle B and unbranded range cattle, and any horses we find, and drive them to Calvert. I saw a notice at the hotel that cattle buyers there were willing to pay $10 gold per head. We would need two hundred head minimum but more likely two hundred and twenty-five to account for any loses and to cover expenses."

Bridges spoke up, "Boss, there's a closer place. John Chisum is gathering a herd on the Concho River near Paint Rock Bluff for a drive to Kansas. Franks and several other ranchers from Lampasas and San Saba like Sam Gholston and John Hitsons are rounding up cattle and selling them to him for $10 per head. He's a lot closer than Calvert."

Ballard nodded and said, "Fine we'll go there." He went on to explain, "We have three problems: One, are there enough cattle and horses to raise the money? Two, can we round them up in time? And three, can we drive them to the Concho River and return in time to prevent the foreclosure?"

These three questions could only be answered in time, but there was another one that had to be answered immediately: Where and how to hold the rounded up cattle. Range cattle were accustomed to drifting in small groups but not in large herds. They wouldn't stay in a herd unless forced.

"Monty, tonight we'll rope-hobble the remuda and turn them out of the corral. They won't go far with the hobbles. Then over the next few days, we'll fill the corral with cattle. It'll hold forty-five to fifty. After that, we'll need something else. Bridges, do you know where there is a small box canyon somewhere with some grass and water and on the Circle B?"

"Yes, boss, there's two or three, but I think I know the one you want. It's where Cherry Creek runs into Little Saline. Cherry Creek starts at a spring at the head of a canyon. The canyon is only four or five hundred yards long and it's narrow at the mouth."

"Good. Are there some trees and quite a bit of brush around the mouth?"

He nodded yes.

"What we'll do," Ballard said, "is make a brush fence across the canyon mouth to hold the remaining cattle for a short time during the roundup. I figure it's about seventy-five to ninety miles to the Concho River and that should take seven to ten days, depending on the terrain and how fast we get the cattle trail broke. That would give us a little over two weeks to finish the roundup. The return trip will cut into that a little. It could be done in one day, but it would probably kill a horse so we're really talking two days and that leaves us out on a limb and pressed for time. Any questions, thoughts, or ideas?"

Bridges said, "Boss, I think I'll bake up enough biscuits tonight to last two weeks and we've got enough jerky to last the same, so each person should be responsible for his own food. I'll be too busy to cook if we're going to finish this job."

"You're right. Everyone is on their own as far as food is concerned. Now, if there's nothing else, we better get our gear ready to go because daylight comes early."

It was still dark when they rode out of the ranch yard, and they heard the first cattle before they could actually see them. Soon the gray light of early dawn penetrated the blackness and horns began to flash above the brush. These cattle closer to the house seemed accustomed to humans because by noon they had located and driven into the corral eighteen head. Three days disappeared in a blur of cactus, thorns, dips, dodges, ropes, curses, and cracked lips. At dark of the third day, there were forty-two head in the corral. The last ten or twelve had been the wildest and hardest and had to be roped and dragged every foot of the way to the corral. The top of the barn was full of hay and each day Ballard forked down so much they couldn't eat it all. The hay accomplished two things—first, hungry cows are edgy and nervous so it calmed them down, filled them up, and made them lazy; and second, as Ballard worked forking it into the corral, they got used to his human smell and lost some of their wildness.

There was twenty head of unbranded range cattle in the group. Ballard decided to brand them immediately. He was planning to move to a new location the next day because there weren't many cattle left near the headquarters, and he wanted these branded before the move. In any event, they had to be branded before they left Circle B land. They might stampede and scatter on someone else's range and have to be rounded up again. People rounding up unbranded cattle on someone else's range have been hung. In addition, John Chisum would want a bill of sale and would only pay for branded cattle.

So Ballard, Bridges, and Monty worked until well after midnight, building the fire, heating the irons, roping, dragging, tying. There was the smell of burned hair and skin in the night air, cows and calves were bellowing. Afterwards they fell into their bunks only to rise again before first light, not fully awake, just going through the motions of saddling and riding. Bridges brought the wagon because they had to have their bed rolls and everything they'd need because they wouldn't be back until the task was finished. Before they left, Ballard forked enough hay to the penned cattle to last them for at least a month, and water from the house spring ran through one corner of the corral so it was no problem.

They arrived at the junction of Little Saline and Cherry Creeks about mid-morning. Cherry Creek canyon was just as described, and there were already two cows and a half-grown calf grazing in it. As Bridges set up camp, Monty and Ballard began to cut brush to fence the canyon mouth. There was an ample supply, and by noon they had dragged up and tied together enough to block the canyon mouth to a height of about six feet. Ballard purposely left a gap between two oak trees. These two trees were about twenty-five feet apart and would form the entrance. Ballard decided they would use a rope gate and would pull the wagon parallel at night to reinforce it. The last thing they did was build two arms of brush leading diagonally away from each of the gate oaks to form sort of a chute or funnel. Cattle have a sixth sense. They seem to know when you're putting them somewhere they can't escape from, and the moment they recognize it they'll try anything to get away. With the chute they'd have to jump six feet of thorny brush or run over a horse and rider to get away.

Again, Ballard and his crew threw themselves into the work. The thickets, draws, and canyons all held cattle, and the only way to get them out was to plunge in head first and drive or drag them out. Brush slapped your face, limbs tried to knock you out, thorns scratched and poked, the sun blazed, snakes rattled, horses bucked, fingers bled from handling the rope, and the dust never settled, but the work was slowly getting done . . . maybe too slowly.

Sundown of the fifth day they matched their tallies. Ballard had brought in thirty-six head, Monty thirty-nine, and Bridges twenty-eight. There were three already in the canyon, so they had a total of one hundred and six here and forty-two back at the headquarters. The supply in the area was still plentiful, but eight days had passed and Ballard calculated they had only four left to round up another eighty head, brand those that needed it, and hit the trail. Time was short, very short. They needed a break.

They got it the next morning. Ballard was riding down a dry creek following the sound of a bawling calf when he broke out into a pretty green canyon. From where he sat, he could see twenty-five or so head peacefully grazing under the watchful eye of an old mossbacked herd bull. He must have weighed 2000 pounds, stood six foot at the shoulders, and his horns were at least four foot long and as big around as Ballard's leg. Most of the other stuff appeared to be one or two years old, but several were mature cows with calves at their sides.

Ballard wheeled his horse and returned to camp just as Monty drove a cow and calf through the gap. While Ballard was waiting for Monty to latch the gate, Bridges rode up dragging a small bull that they all hazed through the entrance. Ballard explained the situation and they rode back to the small canyon.

When they arrived, the bull spotted them immediately. He was standing on a small knoll and he began to paw the ground, throwing dirt on his back, shaking his horns from side-to-side, and glaring at them with suspicious eyes. Bridges cut across in front of him toward the herd and with a bellow of rage, the bull lowered his head and charged. Bridges' horse moved away with the bull in close pursuit. Ballard and Monty had each shaken out a loop as soon as the bull charged. While his attention was diverted, they bolted their horses up behind and each dropped a noose over his head and then rode out to either side. Target and the dun Monty was riding put on their brakes, sliding to a stop, and the bull, realizing his mistake, turned with a roar.

By this time, it was too late. Both horses were experienced cow ponies and when the bull tried to charge one horse, the other held firm and even tried to drag him back, and when he turned the other way, the same thing happened. While he was so occupied, Bridges rode up and cast a third loop over his horns from the rear and the trap was complete. Now, they had him where they could manage him without getting killed.

Monty and Ballard turned their horses and headed back out the dry creek. They started off well apart with Bridges directly behind. The bull couldn't charge in any direction, so he shook his massive head and followed. However, there was still fire in his eyes. Turning around in his saddle, Ballard was overjoyed to see the other cattle trailing along behind.

Sometimes it's harder to let something go than it is to catch it, so when they got near the gap, Ballard made sure this didn't happen. He stopped at a tree a good rope's length from the gap and removing the lariat from his saddle horn tied it to the tree trunk, while Monty and Bridges held tight. Then Ballard rode over and removed the gate and returned to tie the rope back to his saddle horn. They led the bull into the valley, and once he and the rest of the trailing cattle were all through the gate, Ballard rode up to another tree and this time Monty rode around to join him but on the opposite side of the trunk, with Bridges still behind the bull. Ballard and Monty backed their horses up until the bull's head was against the tree and then rode around the tree in opposite directions tying him to the tree. Bridges dropped his rope and they all breathed a sigh of relief.

They rode back through the gate and as they did Ballard counted thirty-two cattle that had followed their patriarch from the valley. With the other ten brought in that morning they now had a total of one hundred and ninety. Working hard the remainder of the day, they were able to raise the number to two hundred and two.

The morning of the tenth day it was pouring down rain. High thunder clouds were building, lightning flashed across the sky, not just one bolt at a time but three, then four, then two. God was putting on quite a show. There was a constant rumble of thunder with an occasional shattering boom. The rain fell in sheets and the ground was a swamp.

The cattle were milling around back and forth looking for a way out. The wagon blocked the entrance, but Ballard was worried. A panic stricken herd can run over anything. Ballard and the other two rode inside and closed the gate, pulling the wagon back in place. Each patrolled a section of the fence. Suddenly, a bolt of lightning struck near and then another. The herd bolted. Out they came, the devil at their tail. Jumping Target directly toward the leaders, Ballard whipped his yellow slicker in their faces and fired his pistol at their feet. Monty and Bridges were doing the same. Relentlessly, the cattle pushed them back. They gave ground grudgingly. Target's hindquarters were in the thorny brush when they finally began to turn away. As they did, Ballard pounced, slapping, yelling to keep them moving, staying to their outside, pushing them in a large circle like a wheel. An hour passed and the cattle were finally exhausted, the storm was spent, and the herd finally began to quiet. The crisis had passed.

It remained dark and cloudy the rest of the day and it was too slick to go out. The eleventh day dawned sunny, and Ballard and his crew threw themselves into the saddles and were able to bring their total to two hundred and twenty-three. Of that two hundred and twenty-three, there were approximately forty that needed branding. Once this was done, all these cattle would have to be driven to the ranch house, the other cattle picked up, plus ten horses, which Ballard thought he would be able to sell, and the drive would start for the Concho River.

It took two days to complete the branding. The morning of the fourteenth day was clear. Monty and Ballard saddled their horses, while Bridges hitched up the wagon. The rope gate was removed and they rode to the old longhorn bull tied to the tree. Ballard dismounted, and carefully reaching around the tree, cut Bridges' rope. Ballard and Monty picked up their ropes and rode around the tree in opposite directions, releasing the bull. First, they led him to water for a drink and then started for the entrance. He had learned his lesson well and followed like a dog. The other cattle, just like they were supposed to, trailed along behind. As they left the entrance, the wagon was on one side of the herd. Ballard and Monty were in the lead. Monty rode over and handed Ballard his rope. It was a gamble, but it worked as the bull tamely continued to follow. After watching him for a few moments, Monty dropped back on the opposite side of the herd from the wagon.

They continued in this manner until afternoon and then Ballard decided to try an experiment. It had to be done sooner or later anyway. He waved Monty over and handed him his rope. They rode on opposite sides of a tree and repeated the performance of tying the bull. Ballard then dismounted and edged up to the tree, cutting both ropes and freeing the bull. He was now completely unrestrained—would he charge? The other cattle were patiently waiting for the outcome. The bull watched Ballard as he approached on horseback, but as Target stepped in his face, he turned and resumed his lead at the head of the herd. It continued to work that way until just at dark they arrived at the main headquarters.

— Chapter Twelve —

North to the Concho

THEY UNLOADED THE WAGON that night. It would stay behind; Bridges' donkey would pack their supplies. The donkey was trained and would follow without being led. This would free Bridges to herd, and they would need all three hands if they were to make Chisum's camp.

Monty drew the bobtail watch and stayed with the herd until midnight. Ballard relieved him and stayed the remainder of the night. First light of the fifteenth day found Ballard throwing open the corral gate and pushing the cattle out to where Monty and Bridges were waiting to escort them to the main herd. These penned cattle were sleek from the immense amount of hay they had been stuffing down. They shuffled over to the others meek as kittens.

Now, the tense moment came. Ballard again rode toward the lead bull, wanting him to turn and head out north toward the Concho River. The bull lowered his head, shook his horns, but as Ballard neared thought better and wheeled and walked north. Bridges and Monty were on the flanks slapping cattle with their ropes, hollering, "Get up, get up, moo cow, moo cow, head out, go on, head out."

Slowly the herd started moving and strung out in a sort of pear shape behind the lead bull. As they started, Ballard estimated they were about nine miles northwest of Three Forks and thirty miles south and a little east of Menardville. Paint Rock on the Concho River was about seventy-five miles due north, but before they reached it, he knew they would have to deal with numerous creeks, the San Saba River, and some of the roughest and most inhospitable country known to man.

They now had thirteen days to reach their destination and two days to get the money back to Chester Roberts.

— Chapter Thirteen —

Apache Raiders

THE APACHE KNELT AROUND the fire in the center of the large hogan. Nana, war chief of the Minbreno Apaches, lifted his eyes with the rising smoke and began to pray. "Usen, great father of the Apache, hear our prayer. Once we were many. Our enemies slept with weapons in hand, their women cried in the night. Now, we are few. The pale eyes hunt us, kill our women and children, steal our land. They are numerous as leaves that fall from the trees in winter. Without your help, the Apache are doomed. Tomorrow it will be the full moon, and we again go to attack the white man. Give us a sign you will ride with us."

The medicine man rose, sleek copper shoulders above a deep barrel chest. He began a slow ceremonial circle dance. A dozen savage faces watched. His body was painted a greenish brown; upon his back were white zigzag lines of lightning, twisted around each arm a yellow snake, and on his breast a great standing red bear. He wore the horned head of the great white buffalo. Tied into his twin braids were the rattles of the rattlesnake, in one hand was a hoop covered with horsehide. Dangling from the hoop's rim were eagle feathers. As he danced, he twirled the leather cover hoop to ward off evil spirits. In his other hand was a skull shaker filled with bone and gunpowder. Each time he whirled past the fire, it flared, the orange and yellow flashing off the copper faces of the watchers.

He was chanting, "Hear our prayer, Usen, hear our prayer." Suddenly the entrance flap of the hogan was thrown back. All eyes turned to the warrior who entered. "Nana, the pale eyes with a great herd of cattle and some horses cross our land." The warriors were not surprised. It was not the first time Usen had answered their prayers.

Nana rose. "Sharpen your knives, make many arrow points, and ready your horses. Tomorrow we ride against the intruders."

Later that night, Running Antelope came limping up to Nana. Nana had hoped this would not happen but had known in the back of his mind it would. "Father," he said, "I am now fifteen summers old. It is time I went on my first raid. Others ride with you who are my age."

It was true, Nana could not deny it. But the other young warriors did not have a twisted leg. Usen's back had been turned when Running Antelope was born and one of his legs was twisted like the trunks of the cedar high on the wind-swept cliffs. Nana did not care. He loved his son, loved him much more than a war chief should love anything. This was his only child and somehow he knew there would never be another. So all his love, saved for the many children of a large family, was showered on his son.

"Be patient, my son. There are enough white men to last for many more raids."

"But father, I have asked many times. The son of a war chief must be an example. How can I be if I never take the warrior's path to steal the horse, to fight our enemies?"

Nana's heart swelled with pride. He knew courage dwelt in his son, but he steeled himself and said, "My word is final. You stay behind and guard the camp."

Running Antelope turned without a word and dejectedly limped off. He went directly to his secret place in the woods, a cave under a deadfall. Here he pulled out his quiver of arrows and looked at each one, making sure the points and feathers were firmly attached. Next, he got his bone-handled knife and stroked it on his leggings until it was razor sharp. Finally, he got his hair hackamore and checked it. It would need to be strong to guide his war pony. He went to the field where the horses grazed, whistled up his paint pony and took him to water, and then tied him to the old tree near his secret place.

He had never defied his father, but he knew that when the war party left in the morning, he would not be far behind.

— Chapter Fourteen —

Dogs, a Bear, Wolves, and Longhorn Cattle

THE TWO BORDER COLLIES, Bingo and Banjo, knew something was terribly wrong. All their lives they had been trained to do one thing, as their fathers, and fathers' father before, till the beginning of their line—to protect, to hold, to keep their wooly wards safe. If the coyote, wolf, lion, or bear came, they fought, and fought, and sometimes died but never gave up, never let the sheep be taken. Always before when danger threatened, the master would come with the stick of fire. Its thunder hurt their ears, but hurt the wild ones more for they fell dead when it spoke.

But now, something was wrong. Two days ago, the copper men who smelled of the earth and of the fire smoke came and took the sheep. The master's stick thundered, but the whistling limbs flew and he fell and had not moved for two days. With no sheep to watch, they watched their still master. He didn't need herding, but the great black birds, which kept trying to land on him did. So Bingo and Banjo jumped and snapped at the birds each time they came near. At first, there were only two or three, but now, there were a dozen circling slowly overhead.

Bingo wanted to leave, to follow the trail of the sheep, but Banjo wanted to stay. Banjo was the older and Bingo always deferred to his will. So, she impatiently laid down in the shade of a bush, her head rested on her two front legs. She was the first to feel the ground shake ever so slightly, then more, almost like when the great buffaloes ran in fear, but not the same, not so many hooves, not so big. The bushes moved on the other side of the clearing and she bounced to her feet and barked. Banjo joined her as the lead bull of the cattle herd stepped into sight.

✳✳✳✳✳✳✳✳✳✳✳✳✳✳✳✳✳✳✳✳✳✳✳✳✳✳✳✳✳

The deer dashed from the meadow at the sound of the brush breaking and of the small trees being bowled over. Soon a huge silver-brown shape could be seen hurling down the slope, oblivious to the undergrowth. Like a landslide, he ran over anything in his path. Reaching an opening, he reared up on his hind legs. Standing almost eight feet tall and weighing over a thousand pounds, he looked around with his little red pig eyes.

Not long out of the cave from the long winter's sleep, his sides were hollow, ribs protruding, and he had a ravenous hunger. His day had been spent in digging up two ground squirrels, destroying numerous ant mounds for eggs, and breaking into several rotten trees to eat the grubs. But he was still famished and needed something of substantial size to quiet the rumblings in his stomach. The smell of carrion was in the air and he meant to find it.

He didn't see anything in the valley, but he heard a snarl coming from a thicket further down the slope. With no regard to what it might be, since he feared no living thing, he hurled himself down to the flat land. Bursting into the brush, he spotted a pack of six wolves devouring the remains of a small fawn. Without losing his momentum he threw himself into the pack.

Slapping right and left, his huge paw sent two wolves rolling like cannon balls. Two others he crashed into, turning them several flips. They all scattered like quail. For a moment, the largest two wolves turned back, but the bear, seeing this, let out a terrible roar and they quickly disappeared into the surrounding trees.

After consuming what was left of the half gone fawn, the bear was still hungry, and looking over the valley, he spotted a dozen or so circling buzzards. In his little brain, he knew that where the large black birds circled, there was often food. He set off at a trot in that direction.

****

Walking into the cave the lanky cowboy said, "Ballard's finished the roundup and started the herd north." The biggest of the two men by the fire replied, "Don't matter. They think they're going to sell that herd and pay off the I.O.U. Well, they've got another think coming. The boss says no, and we'll see he's right. We'll stampede that herd, scatter it from hell to breakfast, and then see if there's enough time for three men to round it up again. Besides, if we get lucky, one of them might just catch a stray bullet."

The third man was patiently rolling a cigarette. As he finished, he took a blazing twig from the fire and lit it, dragging smoke deep into his lungs. He looked up with ice blue eyes and said, "Bullets can fly in both directions."

"What's that supposed to mean?" The large man asked. The smoker seemed to consider his answer, looking at the tip of his cigarette. "I've known Monty Flach since he was a kid and he's fought Indians, rustlers, and just to stay alive. He won't be an easy man to back down. In addition, this Bridges is known among the Indians as a dead shot and a tough bastard, and I've heard tell of an Adam Ballard who was working with the Texas Rangers over in the Salt Lake War and was a regular ring-tailed tiger. Went after a killer who shot his friend and rode into Pedro Sanchez's headquarters and shot Sanchez and Ike Bricker to rags."

"Ike Bricker, wasn't he the one who rode with Sam Bass and had fifteen notches on his guns?"

"Yah, he fancied himself fast with a pistol, but he's stone dead now."

"Well, if they're so bad, what do you want to do, turn tail and run?"

"No, all I'm thinking is we better be mighty careful and not underestimate these yahoos if we want to come out of this in one piece."

The men were silent for a few minutes watching the fire, lost in their thoughts. The smoke was drifting out of the cave into a clear starlit night, and the moon was almost full.

The big man finally said, "We might as well hit them tomorrow. It's a rustler's moon and if we have to ride at night, we'll need the light."

The smoker tossed his cigarette into the fire. The horses snorted and moved restlessly behind him. "What's wrong with them horses?"

"Probably smell a bear. I saw tracks down by the creek big as a wash pan, never saw tracks so large. Appears he must have hibernated in this cave this winter. We better keep our Winchesters handy and hope he doesn't come back. The last thing we need is an angry grizzly in the middle of the night."

"Say, as we rode in this afternoon, did you notice the smoke south of here?"

"Yeh. I saw it."

"Probably those damn Apache. Maybe they'll take care of the herd for us."

Again, the smoker looked up, and said, "Or take care of us for the herd."

No one laughed.

— Chapter Fifteen —

Running Antelope's Grizzly Challenge

"HE LOOKS LIKE A pincushion with all those arrows sticking in him, but at least they didn't scalp him," Monty said.

"Yep, thanks for small favors," Ballard replied as he tightened the reins on Target who was dancing nervously at the smell of the dead body.

Ballard was anxious to continue the trail drive, but as he looked at the circling buzzards, he knew they couldn't just leave this body. Noticing a dry wash on his right, he motioned at Monty and said, "We can push him in that little ravine and cave the bank off over him and pile some rocks on top."

This was hurriedly done. In the meantime, Bingo and Banjo had raced to opposite sides of the cattle. Woe to the hapless animal that drifted too far from the herd. Suddenly, a whirlwind of teeth, barks, growls, and nips descended, driving it back.

"Would you look at that," Monty said, as they finished their burial detail. "Looks like we've picked up a couple of new wranglers."

"Yep, who'd have thought sheep dogs would herd cattle! Never would've believed it unless I saw it with my own eyes."

As the cattle moved along, the dogs proved invaluable. Actually, they were better than two hands, because they were quicker and covered more ground. Ballard was now free to scout ahead. It was late afternoon, and he estimated the herd could travel no more than two or three more miles before bedding down for the night.

They were presently moving through fairly open country where grass was sparse. There were flats of chaparral brush, with scattered stands of mesquite and lots of prickly pear. Ballard rode up on a little knobby hill and stopped to watch the cattle below. The setting sun caught the rising dust in its dying rays and made it glimmer like thousands of lightning bugs. The dogs were working back and forth along the flanks of the herd. Bridges was out of sight on the drag and Monty was on the opposite side swinging a rope as he rode.

As Adam Ballard watched, he wondered, have we a chance to make it? Three men and two dogs with over two hundred longhorn cattle that are as fast as deer and just as wild—can we hold them together for the next seventy miles? Where were his enemies? Who were his enemies? He didn't even know that. Was the man with the cracked boot heel around? Would he make another attempt or had he been scared off?

He shivered a little. For all he knew, he could be in the man's rifle sights at this very moment. With these morbid thoughts still in mind, he spurred Target off the hill and headed north.

****

After riding about two miles, Ballard came to a little open valley. Running down the middle was a creek with several pools of deep water. The valley was evidently a watershed for the creek because its lush grass indicated more year-round moisture than the sparse grass of the surrounding territory. Along the banks of the creek were several groves of pecan trees with plenty of wood for a camp fire. The valley tilted slightly from south to north and opened into a large area of thick chaparral and mesquite, an almost impenetrable wall of thick brush. Satisfied he had found the first night's bedding, ground he turned and rode to meet the herd.

That night after the herd was settled, he and Monty were having a cup of coffee, while Bridges and the dogs were standing the first watch.

"Monty, did you see smoke to the southwest just before dark?" Ballard said.

"Yep, boss, it was probably Apache and they're up to no good, bet on that."

"Well, we're safe enough. Apache never attack at night, but we better keep our eyes peeled and pistols handy tomorrow. In fact, we better sleep in our clothes and keep our horses saddled and tied close at hand. Warn Bridges when you relieve him tonight."

"O.K., Boss. Say, would you look at that full moon! Always makes me nervous to see the full moon. Seems everything that works at night becomes busier."

****

Ballard didn't know at the time, but Monty's fears were justified because as he spoke the Apache were moving onto a brushy hill above the camp. Running Antelope who had followed the main band, lost their trail in the dark, and passed between them and the herd and was eating jerky in an arroyo just west of the camp. His horse was tied to a bush and his spirits were high as he daydreamed about the glory of the coming battle.

Two miles north as the crow flies, three men were saddling up. "We'll hit 'em just at daylight. The herd's still green and wild and it'll be well rested. We'll circle to the other side and flush the cattle across their camp into the heavy brush. If they're not trampled to death in the stampede, they'll never get their cows out of the brush. If we get separated, we'll meet back here. Any questions?"

The others shook their heads no.

"O.K., let's ride."

Just at the first pink-gray hint of dawn, Running Antelope noticed his horse getting nervous, and as he moved to quiet him, a shower of small rocks and dirt fell down the side of the arroyo. He turned, and above him sliding down the bank was the largest bear he had ever seen. His horse, with a terrified wrench of its head, broke its hair hackamore and dashed away squealing in fright. The bear reached the bottom and turned toward Running Antelope. Knowing his bow and arrows were useless against this monster, he discarded them and threw his bag of jerky at the bear and turned and ran up the little canyon.

The deerskin bag hit at the bear's feet and he paused to devour the bag, the tie string, the beadwork and the jerky; but it didn't dent his appetite and after licking his lips twice, he followed the limping boy up the ravine.

Running Antelope was in an area of scattered trees, brush, and huge slabs of rock. These boulders had cracked off the cliff above and had fallen in irregular stacks here below. He hobbled into a small grove of trees. The biggest was only eighteen feet tall and about eight inches in diameter; quickly he climbed to its top, and just in time because the bear was right behind, lumbering up to the tree growling and biting large chunks out of its bark.

Realizing he couldn't chew the tree down, the bear rose on his hind legs and slapped at the boy's feet. His great claws tore through the leather moccasins like scissors through paper but missed the feet inside. Running Antelope quickly drew his knees under his chin and out of reach. Seeing he couldn't reach the boy, infuriated the bear and dropping to all fours, he attacked the surrounding bushes and trees, knocking them down, pulling them up, throwing them in all directions, constantly roaring and growling at the top of his lungs. Back he came like a rabid wolf, slobber flying from his mouth, and rising, threw his massive weight against the tree trunk.

Running Antelope was tossed back and forth with such violence that he almost lost his grip. But it didn't seem to make much difference whether he held on or not because the tree slowly began to bend toward the ground. When the end became inevitable, he released his grip and jumped. As he hit, his weak leg gave and he fell. Not bothering to rise, he started crawling toward a small opening between two boulders.

The bear quickly dropped to all fours and closed on the crawling boy. Just as Running Antelope squeezed through the hole, he felt a searing pain rake along the calf of his leg, but wrenching free he pulled out of the way. Instantly, the bear's face filled the opening, which was too small for him to enter. Roaring his outrage at being cheated out of a meal, he reached his paw into the cavern. The boy was flattened against the very back wall and the bear's claws were within a hair of his feet. They raked big grooves in the dirt near his toes.

As the bear reached again, Running Antelope pulled his knife and as the claws crept closer he struck. Dead into the center of the paw he drove the blade. A deafening roar of rage and pain filled the cave as the bear chewed and gnashed his great fangs on the rocks around the entrance. Drops of hot saliva showered the boy as the boulders shook under the bear's angry onslaught. But even the bear's massive strength was no match for these heavy giants.

For several minutes, the bear licked his paw and glared at the boy. Finally, he rose and disappeared from sight. Blood was beginning to pool underneath Running Antelope; he was getting weak, and dots were floating before his eyes. He knew he had to get help soon or bleed to death. But was the bear gone?

Looking around the little cave, he spotted a stick about fifteen inches long and an inch around. He took off his red flannel head band and tied it to the end of the stick. Leaning over but staying as far from the entrance as possible, he reached with his left hand and pushed the stick through the opening. Nothing. He waved it back and forth, still nothing. He moved closer and pushed it out further.

Smash! A heavy paw thundered down as the bear crushed the stick and reached into the cave. Running Antelope was fast and almost got out of the way, but the bear's claws caught in his leather sleeve and he was pulled toward the entrance. His knife was in his right hand and he slashed at the bear. The animal howled in fury and pulled, slamming the boy against the front wall.

Hot, foul bear-breath hit the Indian's face, he was seeing black, and he slashed at the bear again. The great spirit was with him, because even though he missed the bear, he cut the leather that had caught in the bear's claws, freeing himself again. He jumped back and flattened himself against the back wall and the bear, after glaring at him, first with one eye and then the other, decided to look for easier game and moved off toward the sound of mooing cattle.

Running Antelope picked up the stick and put the head band around his injured leg, and used the stick to twist it tight until the bleeding stopped. He tied the stick in place with a piece of leather from his shirt and lying back closed his eyes and drifted into a restless sleep.

— Chapter Sixteen —

The Bull and the Bear

BALLARD AND MONTY WERE fixing breakfast when Bridges came riding up leading a paint pony.

"Say, Boss, something's bad wrong up that ravine on the west side of the herd. This Indian pony just came out of there like he was going for the Rio Grande. He's got a broken hackamore and he's trembling and scared to death. Maybe we'd better go have a look-see."

They swiftly mounted and headed toward the ravine, with Bridges leading the pony. While they were still four hundred yards away, their horses threw up their heads, snorted, and stopped dead in their tracks. Monty was thrown clear over his horse's head but fortunately held his reins, his horse rearing and rolling his eyes wanted to run. Bridges' horse had turned in a complete circle and was facing the opposite direction but wildly looking over his shoulder. The paint pony had pulled from his grip and disappeared into the brush.

Target was dead still, head high. Suddenly a giant bear burst from the ravine entrance and threw himself in a beeline for the cattle. Ballard whipped out his rifle and spurred his horse, but Target slid sideways as if he had hit an invisible wall. Back and forth he went but forward was not in his language.

As the bear charged, cattle were scattering in panic but not quite fast enough, as the bear swatted a half grown calf, knocking it dead with a skull-shattering blow. He was so obsessed with the great hunks of flesh he was tearing from his victim and swallowing that he never saw the longhorn bull, which hit him like a locomotive under a full head of steam. The bull's head took the bear full in the back and his momentum carried him under the bear and he flipped him over his head. The bear hit the ground with a resounding crash and the bull whirled and tried to gore it from the side. The bear, however, was equally fast and rose on his hind legs, pulling his forelegs and head out of the way. Still, as the bull passed, his razor-pointed horn raked a gash across the bear's stomach.

Again, the bull whirled, but this time he stopped, facing the roaring bear. The bear turned his snout to the sky and his outraged growls shook the surrounding hills. But as he looked at the unimpressed longhorn bull, his little brain for the first time in his life held doubt, which is the mother of fear. He was hurt, probably several broken ribs as well as a deep gash across the front of his body, and there across from him unhurt, unbloodied, stood his enemy snorting, bellowing, and pawing the ground, throwing great clods of dirt into the air.

Again, the bull charged. This time the bear struck him a thundering blow to the head, but as he was knocked sideways, he kept driving and he hooked a horn into the bear's leg. They swung in a circle and the bear jumped on the bull's back, biting at his neck. Down on the ground they went, a rolling ball of horns, teeth, hooves, and claws. The noise was deafening and the dust was so thick Ballard couldn't tell what was happening. Target, head high, eyes unblinking, was trembling, and so was Ballard. The force and sound were terrifying for man or beast to witness.

Suddenly they parted, facing each other, growling, roaring, bellowing, and bleeding. Ballard could see great claw marks on either side of the bull's back, one of his ears hung in tatters, but the bear was also bleeding from several places and seemed to be favoring his left leg. Neither showed the slightest desire to cease hostilities. Again, they met in shattering crash of bodies but as they did, the cattle herd, which had been nervously watching from a good distance, bolted straight toward both the warriors and Ballard and his crew.

At first Ballard couldn't understand why the cattle were coming and then he heard shots and knew the herd was being stampeded. Waving at Monty and Bridges to follow, Ballard wheeled and ran for his life. As he turned, he glimpsed the herd boil over the two combatants and they were completely lost to sight. Ballard and his crew managed to skirt the charging herd and crossed the creek out of the way. The herd went right over their camp and hit the brush going full tilt.

Ballard breathed a sigh of relief because everyone was alive, but realistically he knew they would not be able to retrieve the cattle, and it looked like the ranch was lost. Someone will pay for this, he thought, as he motioned at his crew, and spurred up the valley.

As they rode, Ballard noticed there was no sign of the bull or the bear. Reaching the head of the valley, they rode in widening circles looking for signs. Ballard heard a small cry in the ravine from which the bear had come. Remembering the paint pony, Ballard waved at Bridges and Monty to ride with him and headed up the arroyo. They passed bushes and trees that had been torn up by their roots, and bear tracks were all around. As they neared the head of the little canyon, Ballard called out; nothing was in sight, he listened carefully, but there was no sound. Thinking his hearing had deceived him, he was turning to leave when he heard a moan. Glancing almost at Target's feet, Ballard noticed a small opening between two boulders and sticking out was a small bloody hand clutching a hunter's knife.

Dismounting, Ballard removed the knife from the limp fingers and he and Monty carefully pulled the young Indian from the cavern. The boy had a tourniquet below the knee of one leg on which there were deep claw marks, and he was unconscious from pain or loss of blood. The other leg was twisted and gnarled, and it looked like it had been that way since birth. Ballard got the medical supplies out of his saddlebag and took water from his canteen and carefully washed the wound. Each time the pressure was loosened on the tourniquet one of the wounds bled profusely. It was deeper than the slashes—almost a puncture.

"Monty, would you please build me a fire?" While he did so, Ballard finished cleaning the wounds and poured whiskey on each in the hope of killing any infection. Once the fire was built, Ballard heated the boy's knife blade until it was red hot and then laid it across the puncture, searing the flesh, cauterizing the hole, and stopping the bleeding.

Bridges said, "Boss, we've got company."

Ballard looked up on the sides of the arroyo and there stood twenty or so heavily-armed Apache. He carefully laid the knife aside and said, "Boys, don't make any fast moves or we're dead meat."

Then he turned his attention back to the boy. He finished washing the boy's wounds. As he finished, one of the Indians slid down the side of the arroyo, and roughly pushing Ballard out of the way picked the boy up and walked out of the ravine. The rest of the Apache had their bows and arrows half raised, and Ballard knew the next few moments would decide whether he and his crew lived or died. The Apache mounted his horse with the boy in his lap, and sat facing them for what seemed like an eternity. Once Ballard thought he saw the Indian's hand move to brush hair from the little brave's face, but knew he must have been mistaken for Apaches never showed any sign of tenderness or love, especially in front of their enemy. Suddenly, the Apache turned his horse away and spoke over his shoulder. Ballard's heart leaped to his throat. Was it life or death?

As if in answer, the Apache lowered their weapons, turned reluctantly away, and disappeared from view. Monty weakly sat down on a rock and Bridges took a large bandana from his rear pocket, wiped sweat from his face, and said, "I've been up the hill and over the mountain and I fought Indian and whites, but I don't think I've ever been closer to death."

— Chapter Seventeen —

The Killing Field

THE THREE RIDERS PULLED up outside the cave.

"Let's get our gear and hit the trail back."

"Yep, the boss'll be happy at the way those cattle scattered in the brush. They'll never get 'em out."

"Too bad about the bear and bullfight. If not for that, they'd been in camp when those cows tromped through."

The horses were restless and pulling nervously on the reins.

"Whoa, whoa boy. What's gotten into them horses?"

"They must still smell the bear that was living here before us."

"Yeh, yeh, well, let's get the stuff and beat it. Ballard and his crew probably aren't far behind us."

They dismounted and started for the cave entrance, but turned as their horses snorted and suddenly ran off, dragging their reins. A terrible premonition seized them and as they turned back to face the cave, it was justified, because from the cave with a rush came the monster bear.

People who know, say a bear can run as fast as a horse, and this bear did nothing to disprove that legend. The cowboys' hands streaked for their pistols as the grizzly came full tilt at the first intended victim. The first shooter fanned the hammer of his weapon rapidly firing until the gun clicked empty. Although all six slugs hit the bear, he didn't flinch or slow down. He hit the man like a shaggy avalanche killing him with a single blow and sweeping on in a scrambled run toward his second target.

The second man also emptied his pistol into the bear. As the slugs hit, the beast growled in savage rage and came on the run. The man realizing what was in store for him wet his pants, threw his pistol aside, and tried to climb over a large rock to get away. The bear rushed up behind the climber swatting him to the ground with one blow. The man drew a knife and as the creature raked him toward its terrible mouth stabbed it into the bear's side. The grizzly broke the man's neck with a chopping blow and clamping his fangs on the dead man's skull literally tore his head off.

The third man was firing deliberately with both handguns. Almost mechanically, he would extend one and fire, and then the other. He appeared almost calm. As the bear came his way, he methodically emptied both guns. The last two shots were muffled by the closeness of the animal's body. By then, the bear had him in a bone-crushing hug, and they fell with the grizzly on top.

Now, all was quiet. Four bodies littered the killing field and not a single heart was beating. Later a pair of camp-robber jays flew into a nearby tree and began to scold at the scene. Eventually, the winged scavenger of the sky began to circle overhead.

****

After the Indians left, Ballard and his crew headed back to assess the damages. Their supplies were trampled to pieces—no flour, no coffee, nothing left. They could see a few scattered cattle in the brush and Ballard spotted the Indian boy's paint pony in a small clearing. Shaking out a loop, Ballard eased Target into the thicket and was lucky his first throw was true. As the rope settled over the pony's head, he humped his back and jumped stiff-legged a couple of times, but then meekly followed as Ballard led him out.

Ballard picketed the pony on some grass near the water and said, "Let's go. We got some getting even to do." They rode to where the stampede had started and began to cast about for sign.

Bridges sang out first, "Here they are."

Sure enough, as Ballard and Monty rode over they spotted the tracks of several shod horses.

"Well, that proves it wasn't the Indians. Indians ride unshod horses. Looks like three of them," Bridges said. Following the tracks they rode in silence for a couple of miles. The first sign of trouble was a saddled horse standing head down on the trail. He was lathered and looked like he'd run a good way.

Monty said, "Boss, look at his reins. They're all broken off on the ends and his mouth is bleeding. He's been running and stepping on his reins. Something must have scared him to death."

Dismounting, they poured water from a canteen into Monty's hat and after giving the horse a drink tied him to a nearby tree; they then back-tracked him almost a mile to the point where he came down off a slope at a dead run.

Ballard saw several buzzards circling overhead. Tying their horses, they took their rifles, spread out, and cautiously crept up until they came to a scene of carnage few could have imagined. Three dead men and a bear lying in pools of blood. Large pools like mud puddles. Ballard never knew humans had so much. One man had the top of his head torn off and the bear was on top of another with his teeth still locked on the victim's throat.

After throwing several rocks at the bear to make sure he was really dead, they approached. One of the first things Ballard noticed was that one of the feet sticking out from under the bear had a boot with a cracked heel. In Ballard's mind, there was not much sympathy for these men. They lived by the ambush and they deserved to die the same way.

"Search them. See if we can find out whose behind this mess."

They emptied the dead men's pockets but other than a few coins, two pocket knives, and a feed store receipt made out to a Tom Jeffers, there was nothing.

"They don't deserve it, but let's find a way to bury them."

They had no tools, but looking in the cave Monty found a smaller cavern that could be sealed by rolling rocks across the entrance. What proved much harder than the burying was moving the bear enough to get the dead bushwhacker out from under him. All three pushed and pulled to no avail, then two pushed on the bear while one pulled on the man, but this didn't work either. Finally Monty and Bridges got two large tree limbs, and using them as levers, pried up one side of the bear. After several attempts Ballard was finally able to pull the man out.

While they worked, Ballard was amazed to note how many wounds the bear had. In addition to a knife sticking out of his rib cage, he could count more than thirty bullet holes, some much larger wounds probably from the bullfight, and one knife wound right through the middle of his paw. It was no surprise when they checked the dead men's pistols that not one contained a live shell, only empty hulls.

As they were sealing the smaller cavern, Ballard noticed a supplies pack in the corner of the larger cave and checking it out found coffee, bacon, flour, a coffee pot, jerky,—replacements for all the things they had lost in the stampede. In addition, there was $700 in gold, and Ballard knew Linda would be mighty happy to get hers back. He was confident $200 of this was what had been taken from her and the other was probably bounty for the dirty work they'd done.

Ballard saw there were two tins of coffee. Shaking one, he realized it was only half full, so he opened the can and poured in the gold, then poured the coffee from the other can over the coins. Then he put both cans with the others in the bottom of the pack. They carted the packs down the slope, mounted, and rode back to the ambusher's horse.

Using tie strings, Ballard made a simple pack over its saddle and said, "Monty, you and Bridges see if you can find the other horses those guys were riding."

While they were doing this, Ballard rode back to the cave and began to skin the bear. It was no easy task. The bear was so large he had to leave the skin across the chest and stomach because he couldn't roll the enormous beast over. After he finished the skinning, he lifted one of the heavy paws and placed it on a flat rock. Pulling each claw out as far as possible Ballard sliced the flesh above and below until he could twist it off. He repeated this on each foot. The claws once removed looked like curved knife blades—fully six inches long they were at least two inches thick at the base. Ballard untied his bandana and dropped them in the center, tying the top in a knot. He put them in his saddle bag, returned to the bear, and folding over the tough skin as best he could, he carried and dragged it down part way to the horses. He dropped it about ten feet from the horses and they pulled, reared, snorted, and threatened to go berserk. Gradually, as Ballard talked to them, they calmed down, and he dragged the skin close, patting their necks, talking softly. Finally, it was right at their feet and after a few minutes of stomping and smelling, they were calm enough for him to tie it on the extra horse and ride back to camp.

Ballard picketed the horses and sat on a log by the creek. Taking each claw from his handkerchief, he used his knife to drill a small hole through the base. By the time Bridges and Monty returned leading the two saddle horses, Ballard had all the claws strung on a leather tie string and back in his saddlebag.

"What are we going to do, Boss—give up, lose the ranch?"

"No, damn it all, we're going to round up as many cattle as we can, find any horses we can, and finish our trail drive. We'll still lose the ranch, but at least we'll have something for our trouble. Now, I've got something to do, so if you two will set up camp and get started on the roundup, I'll be back as soon as possible."

Ballard didn't want to tell them his plan because, first, they would have insisted on going, or, second, they would have tried to talk him out of it. After they rode off, Ballard saddled Target and tied the bearskin on the paint pony and rode to the place he had last seen the Indians.

Their trail was plain and he didn't think they would travel far with the injured boy. After about an hour, Ballard heard a bobwhite call to his left and it was answered on his right and he knew these weren't really quail. As he pulled up, two warriors materialized out of the brush. They both had rifles in the crook of their arms and one waved Ballard to continue as he was.

As Target walked, the Apache trotted along a little behind. They hadn't gone far when they emerged into a clearing by a stream. Several lean-to's made of brush, blankets on the ground, and two camp fires were spread around. All the warriors were standing facing Ballard, and he recognized the one who had carried the boy away—his father, Ballard guessed.

Ballard spurred in his direction, stopped, and dismounted. Taking the lead rope for the paint from his saddlehorn, he handed it to the Indian. The Apache took it, but stepped to the side and Ballard saw the boy lying on a blanket with a deerskin around his shoulders. His face was pale, but his eyes were open and when he saw the pony, a smile touched his lips.

Ballard was watching the face of the boy's father and it seemed to soften as the boy smiled. Turning back, Ballard untied the bear hide and spread it in front of the boy. It was as large as two of their blankets, and Ballard heard the Apaches muttering in amazement at its size. Ballard reached in his saddlebag and withdrew the bearclaw necklace and held it above his head until every eye stared at the claws. Kneeling, he placed it around the boy's neck. Rising, he spread his arms above his head for attention.

Ballard didn't know if they understood English but he said, "This bear, bigger than many buffalo, meaner than the snarling wolf, is now dead, but before he died, he was first wounded by the Apache warrior to whom I have given his skin and claws. When I found this warrior, he was unconscious from his wounds, but clutched in his hand was his knife with a bloody blade. Later, when I skinned the bear, I found the wound inflicted by his knife. This warrior's leg may be withered, but beating in his chest is the heart of the mountain lion."

Lowering his arms, he glanced at the boy's father and saw open pride in his face and knew he understood. The boy's father held up his arm and spoke in Apache at length. Although Ballard didn't understand what the

Indian said, he figured he was translating Ballard's speech. When the Indian finished, Ballard remounted and rode slowly away.

When he got back to camp, it was just dark; but by the firelight he could see some forty to fifty cattle, the donkey, and several horses being herded by the dogs. Ballard had forgotten all about the dogs.

"How in the world did you manage to find these cattle?"

"Oh, we didn't do much. We went into the brush and roped a few horses and were leading them out when we came to a clearing and the dogs were there holding this herd calm as could be."

"Did you see any others?"

"Sure, boss, but it's so thick in there we'll never get them out. Why, we'd need ten or fifteen more wranglers to round them up."

"Well, there's nothing we can do about it tonight. Let's hit the sack. I'm exhausted."

— Chapter Eighteen —

Chisum's Paint Rock Cattle Circus

THE NEXT MORNING AS they were preparing to ride out, Ballard heard a loud bellowing and saw the old longhorn bull with the herd.

"So, he wasn't killed by the bear?"

"No," said Bridges, "It'd take more than a bear to kill that old bull. When we brought the cattle out last night, he was limping along behind, mighty stiff, lots of cuts and scratches, but I think he'll make it."

"Probably a good thing he's not feeling good or we might not be able to keep him with the herd."

By mid-morning, they had dragged, cursed, and driven only six cattle out of the brush. Time and again just when they thought they had two or three, the cattle would cut through or under some brush and escape. They were just too short-handed.

Ballard had just roped a half-grown calf and was dragging him out and thinking how he ought to give this up when Monty rode up and said, "Boss, the Apaches are on a rise west of the camp."

"O.K., come with me."

They dragged the calf to the herd, then rode across the valley to the Indians. As they neared, the boy's father raised his hand with the palm facing them, the universal Indian greeting. When they stopped, the Apache spoke.

"Your people and my people will always be enemies, and yet when the sun rose this morning, there was joy in my heart. My son Running Antelope is now a man. The story of his battle with the bear will be told and retold as long as my people gather around their fires. Much of this I owe to you. From this day forth, you, your family, and men may ride our lands as friends of the Apache." Taking a leather throng with a small bag attached from around his neck, he placed it around Ballard's. "Show this to any Apache warrior and he will do what you ask. This I, Nana, pledge to you. As for today, my warriors and I will help you remove your cows from the brush."

With a wave of his hand, he directed the other Apaches down the slope and into the brush. Soon the valley was alive with the sound of running hooves, shouts, lowing cattle, barking dogs, and breaking brush. By dark that night, Ballard counted two hundred and fifteen cattle in the herd. The Indians disappeared as quietly as they came, never a word, no goodbye, no time for thanks, but Ballard knew as long as the grass grew and the water ran, they would keep their word.

****

The next five days passed without incident and the morning of the twenty-second day found the herd on the south bank of the San Saba River. For two days, Ballard had noticed thunderheads to the northeast and east, and it looked like someone was getting some rain. Now, it was obvious who—the people who lived along the upper reaches of the San Saba—because it was running bank-to-bank. It was a typical Hill Country flood—a heavy rain, then a wall of water. It came quickly and it usually left just as fast. Ballard certainly hoped so because there was no way the herd could cross until the water receded. In many other areas, when water is high, you can still swim a herd across, but in the Hill Country the rivers and even streams are cut down in the bed rock and although in normal times you can ford at just about any point because they are uniformly shallow, when they flood they are so deep you can't cross at all until the water goes down.

The good news was that there was plenty of grass and the cattle were easy to hold against the flooded river. So they waited throughout the first day. Finally, Ballard walked over to the bank and stuck a stick in the mud so he could tell immediately when the water started to recede. Near sundown, the water had moved down about an inch on the stick, but as they were finishing supper it began to sprinkle, then to rain lightly, then to pour. It came in great sheets. Ballard and his crew, including the dogs, were south of the herd holding them against the river. Lightning was spider-webbing across the sky. Occasionally, great bolts hit the ground; before it hit, Ballard could feel the heat, the shock wave, and then the boom. The cattle were panicked, but the wind was blowing from the south and it drove the heavy rain into their faces. They wanted to stampede, but the wind, rain, the dogs, and Ballard and his crew were able to hold them in check until the storm blew out.

The next morning, Ballard's stick was under about a foot of fresh water, and it wasn't until noon of the following day that the water started to recede. Just before dark that night, Ballard was able to walk Target across several times, and he located a solid rock shelf over which the herd could cross.

Dawn of the twenty-fifth day found them fording the river and by ten o'clock they were headed north with about fifty miles still to go to Paint Rock. The herd was trail broke and could cover a lot more territory than when it was green, but they had five days to deliver the herd fifty miles, and they had only covered twenty-five miles in the last seven days. After delivery, they had to turn around and take the money to Three Forks, which would probably take an additional two days. It seemed an impossible task. With this in mind, after the herd was well under way, Ballard rode over to Monty and said, "Hold them in this direction. I'm going to scout ahead and I'll be back tonight. Don't stop until I return."

Heading north, Ballard rode with the contour of the land, between rolling hills, along streams where he could. The land was mostly open although covered with scattered cedar and oaks. After about five miles, he crossed a well-traveled road and thought it was probably the route leading west to Menardville. The country continued the same for the next several miles and when he estimated he had gone the equivalent of two days drive for the herd, he turned back, carefully noting landmarks. All landmarks taken were high points so a man looking up into a night sky would have a good chance of seeing them.

Ballard got back to the herd just at dark and was gratified to see they were about halfway to where he had ridden. Waving Monty and Bridges over, Ballard said, "The trail ahead is clear and we're going to drive straight through tonight. I've marked the trail so we won't stray. Let's change horses and keep pushing these cattle. We're not whipped yet."

They drove through the night and about three in the morning, Ballard saw a hat-shaped rock above a hill to the left and knew this was as far as he had gone. Everyone, including the cattle were exhausted.

Ballard said, "Let the dogs watch them and let's all get some shuteye."

Two hours later, they were on the trail again and night of the twenty-sixth day found them some fifteen miles from Paint Rock.

"Tomorrow I'm going to ride ahead and make the deal with Chisum. As soon as it's done, I'll come back and help you bring the herd on in."

At two o'clock the next day, Ballard rode up on a small hill and saw the sight of a lifetime. Below him on the south side of the Concho River stretched the Chisum herd. Already four or five thousand cattle were gathered, and Ballard could see three distinct camps, each with a large chuck wagon. He estimated there were seventy-five to a hundred cowboys and at least five hundred horses. His herd would only be a drop in the bucket to an outfit like this.

After several moments of watching, Ballard noticed two riders coming to check him out. It made him feel good because no trail boss worth his salt would let a stranger look over his herd without finding out why. As they approached, Ballard immediately liked the gray-haired man who was obviously the leader. You could tell he was used to command, to giving the orders, and to having them obeyed.

He opened with a smile and said, "Don't suppose you'd sell that horse would you?"

Ballard returned the smile and shook his head no, but before he could say anything the man went on, "If you're a cowhand, we can always use another. I'm John Chisum and this is my trail boss, Matt Owen."

Ballard told them his name and neither seemed to recognize it, and went on to say, "No, Mr. Chisum, I'm not looking for work. I've a small herd of cattle a day behind and I'd like to sell. I heard you were buying for a drive to Kansas."

"That's right son. If they're good cattle, properly branded, I'll pay $10 a head gold. How many do you have?"

"I've got two hundred and fifteen cows, more or less—at least that's how many I had when I left this morning. Do you need any horses? I've got ten or so of those I could spare."

"No, not unless they're like that big brute you're on. We're full up, but we sure can use your cows. When will the herd get here? We're thinking of leaving day after tomorrow."

"It's about ten miles behind and we should be able to get it here by noon tomorrow."

"Just right. I'll send some riders to meet you. When you get to my camp, just come to the big tent, right across from the Paint Rock, and we'll settle up. See you tomorrow."

With this he leaned over and shook Ballard's hand and turned and rode back the way he had come. With a shake of his hand he spent over

$2,000, which was a fortune to most men, and now he rode off without a care in the world. Sort of made Ballard a little jealous as he turned and headed south.

The next morning about ten o'clock, six riders loped down a little valley and fell in along the sides of the herd just like they knew what they were doing.

Matt Owens, who was one of them, rode over to Ballard and said, "If you'll ride with me, there's a notch about three miles ahead and the boys are going to string your herd out before they reach it. We'll be on each side to tally the herd and as they pass, I'll also check the brands."

Near noon the herd, strung out to ten times its previous length, started through the notch, and by two o'clock the last cow passed.

Ballard and Owens compared tallies and both had two hundred and fifteen. Owen wrote a note and said, "If you'll take this note to Mr. Chisum, he'll settle with you. As far as we're concerned, the herd is delivered. We'll take it on in." Ballard waved Bridges and Monty over.

"They're taking over from here. Pull over to the side and whistle the dogs up. Pull the remuda out, and put the dogs to herding it. I'm going ahead to pick up the money. Drift the horses south along this trail and I'll catch up with you."

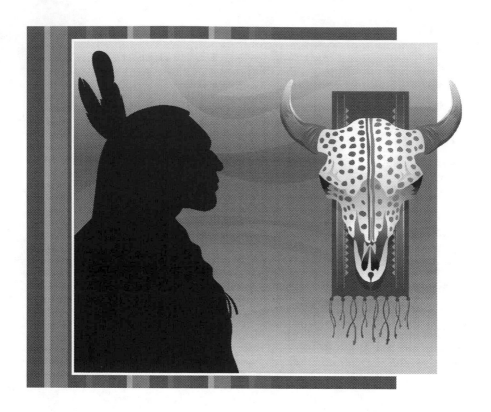

— Chapter Nineteen —

The Best-Made Plans

CHESTER ROBERTS WAITED PATIENTLY for an answer. Finally, Hardin spoke.

"Something's wrong. We'd of heard by now. Either the boys would have sent a message or Ballard would be sulking around with his tail between his legs. I told Jeffers as soon as the herd was stampeded to head for the hidden valley and send word right away."

"I know what you told Jeffers, but it's been two weeks and there's only four days left until the foreclosure, and still no word. What are we going to do about it?"

Both were silent for a moment while the wall clock ticked loudly and finally, made a mechanical noise and struck eight p.m., and then Roberts said, "This is what I think we should do. Send Lanny and six men up to the camp cave. If there's no sign of the boys there, cut north looking for the trail of the herd. It should be plain as day even with the recent rains. As soon as they locate the herd, get it scattered no matter what the cost."

"O.K., it's your money. Consider it done. They'll leave tonight. I'll go see to it now."

"Hardin? One thing more—send a rider to Paint Rock. Have him hire on with Chisum. We may need some eyes and ears at that end." Hardin nodded as he stepped to the door, opened it, slipped through, and was gone.

It wasn't until noon of the second day that an exhausted Rockin M puncher handed Hardin a note in a sealed envelope. Tearing the envelope open, Hardin read: "Jeffers and others dead, herd sold. Will stop Ballard before he gets to Three Forks" and it was signed "L."

Hardin picked up an unused envelope, put the note inside and sealed it. He told the puncher, "Take this to Chester Roberts at the bank."

He leaned back in his chair and wondered what had happened to Jeffers and his other two men. Had he underestimated Ballard? How had Ballard managed to kill three tough men? How did Ballard get his cattle all the way to Paint Rock? None of it made sense at this point, he thought, as he wadded up the torn envelope and threw it at the waste basket. He wasn't surprised when it missed and bounced over behind the door.

* *

Ballard rode into Chisum's camp and made directly for the main tent. It was nearing four o'clock of the twenty-eighth day and he was anxious to finish his business. It took the rider who was stationed at the tent about thirty minutes to locate Chisum and bring him back. Ballard handed him the tally sheet and they walked into the tent. Chisum removed a strongbox from under one of the cots and counted out 110 double eagles. As Chisum finished, Ballard said, "Mr. Chisum, I think you've made a mistake. You gave me $50 too much."

"No, son, I didn't make a mistake. If you had read this note from Matt, you'd have seen that he said to pay you an extra $50 for the lead bull. Appears you've got a trained bellwether bull."

Ballard had to laugh and Chisum looked at him in puzzlement. "Sorry," Ballard said. "If you only knew how much we had to go through to get that bull to lead, and if you had seen the fight he had with a grizzly, you'd know no one in the whole world except lady luck could explain that bull's training."

"Son, this hair got gray watching cattle and I know you just have to accept what lady luck brings and not question. Today she smiled on me and made you laugh out loud so we're both happy."

Shaking his hand, Ballard took the two bags of coins and went outside and put one in each side of his saddlebags. As he was doing this, he looked over Target's rump and saw a scruffy wrangler standing near a buff-colored mustang shortening a stirrup. The wrangler was trying to pretend he didn't even know Ballard was around but doing a very poor job. Twice Ballard glanced up and caught him staring. The next time Ballard looked at the wrangler, he studied him. The man was filthy. One of those people who look dirty even when they're clean. His blond hair hung in matted clumps, his red checked flannel shirt and denim pants were stiff with grease. What was he doing here? Did he work for Chisum? Was he a threat?

Part of Ballard's question was answered as another rider suddenly appeared and said, "Say, you're supposed to be down at Camp Two helping with the branding. This is the third time I've seen you up here. Once more and its all over for you. Now, head on down or hit the road."

The conversation Ballard overheard raised one more question—what was the wrangler doing snooping around up here? Was he after their money, or after Ballard's? Mounting, Ballard rode upward out of the river basin. He passed Matt Owen and his crew bringing the herd in and they exchanged waves. As Ballard reached the crest of the slope, he turned to check his back trail.

As he looked, a commotion broke out on the west side of Chisum's herd. In that area, which was to Ballard's left, a pencil of heavy cedar ran down a draw until it was only about a hundred yards from the main remuda. Indians had used its cover to work down into striking distance and had boiled out and hit the herd, cutting out about sixty horses, and were driving them back up the slope hoping to escape in the gathering dark. A few wranglers were already heading their way, attracted by the shooting between the Indians and the two riders responsible for the remuda. Other cowboys were trying to cut off the remaining four to five hundred horses that had stampeded east. Most of the hands were caught at the evening meal around the chuck wagons, with their horses already turned in for the night. Several of these at the closest camp had drawn their rifles and were pouring heavy fire up the slope after the retreating Indians.

Ballard had to admire the Indians. They seemed to have thought of everything. As the few available riders with horses closed on the disappearing redskins, they ran smack into a rear guard. Unseen, waiting in the cedar, they opened up. Two horses fell end over end, and soon a pitched battle was in progress. Guns flashed like a hundred fireflies and the shots seemed to be a continuous roar. The Indians held for several minutes, and finally, they must have figured the horses were far enough ahead because Ballard saw them break cover and disappear over the crest with the cowboys in hot pursuit.

There was nothing Ballard could do about any of this. Besides, he had plenty of trouble of his own, so he wheeled Target, preparing to head south. As he did so, he caught a glimpse of a rider disappearing into the trees east of his location. Ballard didn't have time to see who it was, but one thing was sure, the horse was buff-colored.

Ballard rode a short distance and the more he thought about the other rider, the more troubled he became. He was certain this was the scruffy cowboy who had been watching him earlier. The wrangler had probably seen the gold and wanted to steal it. If so, he would probably assume Ballard would follow the herd's back trail while riding at night. Then he, or he and some friends, would be waiting somewhere to waylay Ballard.

With this in mind, Ballard pulled off the trail. Dismounting, he untied his bedroll, rolled it on the ground, and removed a pair of heavy wool socks. From his saddlebags, he removed the two leather sacks of gold. He emptied the gold on the bedroll and put a handful of small stones in the bottom of each leather sack. Then he refilled each sack with gold and put them back in his saddlebags.

Over half of the gold still lay on the bedroll. He reached over and pulled some grass and stuffed it into the bottom of one of the socks, then scooped up the remaining gold and poured it in, stuffed more grass on top, and finally tied a knot in the top of the sock. Then he put the whole thing in the other sock, shook it a few times to make sure the coins wouldn't jingle, and rolled it into his bedroll and tied it back behind the saddle.

He remounted and rode on, and had about decided his fears were unwarranted when it happened. Suddenly a shot rang out behind with the bullet humming near his ear.

He spurred Target and the horse bolted. Looking ahead, Ballard could see the notch where the cattle were counted; looking back, he couldn't see anything but he could hear two horses coming fast. Target was running smoothly and Ballard felt good. No horse alive could catch Target, especially at night, when his black color blended in with all the other dark shadows. Besides, these were pretty inept bushwhackers, waiting until Ballard had passed before making their move. Or maybe just wanting him to think they were inept.

As Ballard thought this, he got a sick feeling and turned his face to the front. Target was just entering the notch and Ballard realized this had to be where they were wanting him to go. He hauled back on Target's reins. Too late. A lariat stretched between the rocks hit Ballard chest high. He never saw it until it threw him out of the saddle, crashing to the ground. Dazed, with the wind knocked out of him, he rolled over, drew his pistol, and ran toward the surrounding rocks. A fusillade of shots rang out. Ballard returned fire, twice at one flash and then at another, feeling grim satisfaction at the scream of pain his second return brought. But as Ballard reached the rocks, a gun went off almost in his face and a hammering blow hit his left shoulder.

Despite the wound, Ballard's momentum carried him forward and he crashed headlong into a body, firing his pistol directly into its stomach. As they fell, Ballard's wrist hit a rock and his pistol flew off into the night, Stunned, he groped around on the ground as running steps approached. A bullet bounced off the rock beside him, and he turned to face the danger, but before he could move the night exploded into a rainbow of lights.

Ballard wasn't out long when the sound of someone talking brought him around. His head was a frozen mask of pain and his left shoulder didn't feel too good either.

A voice he recognized from somewhere said, "You're sure he's dead?"

"Yep, I shot him through the head. How long do you think he'll live with a bullet in the brain?"

"O.K., O.K. The boss wanted him dead and I have to ask. Don't get all riled up." "Did you catch his horse?"

"Yes, its over here tied to a tree, a big brute but quiet as a mouse."

"Jennings said he put the gold in his saddlebags, one in each side. Let's just go see."

Then Ballard saw a faint light and guessed they had struck a match.

"Here it is. Strike another match and let me make sure."

Ballard could hear it tinkle as the speaker poured a few of the coins in his hand.

"Yep, looks like it's all here. I'll carry it in my saddlebags. Let's head on back."

"Where's Ike and Joe?"

"Fraid they both bought it. There's only us four."

"Well, tie them over their saddles. We'll leave Ballard here for the buzzards."

"What about his horse?"

"Untie that monster and we'll take him with us."

Suddenly, all hell broke lose, a yell of fear, the sound of tearing cloth, a string of curses, and the sound of a horse's hooves retreating in the distance.

"What happened? What happened? Lanny, are you hurt?"

"His damn, low down, black devil of a horse bit me. He almost took my arm off. I untied him and was putting the reins over the horn when I felt his big teeth clamp on my arm. Before I could move, he had taken a chunk out of me and ran off in the dark."

"Should we go look for him?"

"No, we got what we came after. Let him go."

With this, they mounted up and rode away and Ballard lost consciousness. Some time later, Ballard thought he heard riders passing but was too weak to cry out and fell back into a restless sleep. When he woke again, he could see the first gray hint of dawn. He pulled himself into a sitting position against one of the middle-sized rocks with his legs sticking out in the notch. His wounds burned like he had been branded. His left arm hung useless at his side, so tentatively, he felt the wound near his left shoulder. Actually, it was between his neck and shoulder, about two inches down from the blade, and the bullet had evidently passed through without hitting any bones. He felt somewhat relieved. The slug was out and there were no bone fragments to poison the wound, so maybe he wouldn't die from this one.

Next, he carefully felt his head. Lucky the wound was on the left side so he could reach it with his unwounded arm. It was just above his eyebrow and his fingers shook as he was terrified he'd feel chunks of broken skull or pieces of brain sticking out, but he must have been turning his head when the slug hit, or he had a very thick skull, because it hit above his eyebrow, gouging out a large hunk of flesh, and then slid to the left cutting a grove all the way back over his ear. He had bled profusely and he could understand how anyone touching or looking at him would have thought he was dead.

First, he had to do something about these wounds, then he had to get back to the boys. His mouth was dry, dry as the desert on an August day, so he picked up a pebble and held it in his mouth. After several minutes there was enough saliva and he threw it aside and raising his two fingers to his mouth whistled sharply. He knew training had paid off when he heard the thunder of approaching hooves. Soon, Target's big black shape loomed over him. Target sniffed and snorted at the blood smell but stood patiently. Reaching up with his good arm Ballard grabbed the stirrup and gradually pulled up, easing his feet under him. He was in a squatting position, but the world was spinning and he was too weak to rise. Some minutes passed and the world stopped as he gained strength. Finally, he was able to pull himself to a standing position.

Removing the canteen, he took a small drink and after a few minutes a real thirst-quencher. Putting the canteen back, he untied his bedroll and opened it on Target's rump and was gratified to see the sock of gold still intact. Ballard knew he'd lost the ranch, but at least he had kept this part of the gold from being stolen. He put the gold in his saddlebags and removed the remains of the shirt he had used to bandage the Indian boy. Using his teeth and good hand, he managed to tear off three pieces, leaving the part with the arms. He unbuttoned and took off the shirt he was wearing and laid it across the saddle, and wet one of the rags with water from the canteen and washed his shoulder wounds as best he could. After this, he made a pad with each of the other two small rags, one for the front and one for the back, and using the arms of the shirt, bound the pads over the wounds. Next, he removed his bandana and washed his face, neck, and the area of the head wound, then folding the wet rag into a pad, he bound it in place over the wound with his bandana. He put his shirt back on, taking several minutes to button it with his now clumsy fingers. He didn't bother to try to tuck the tail in—just leaned against Target until he regained a little strength.

His pistol was missing from its holster, and he remembered dropping it, so he looked around but finally realized that even if he spotted it he'd be too weak to pick it up. Gathering his strength he tried to mount, but his legs were lead and he could only lift them halfway up before he slid tiredly back to the ground. He stood for a few minutes gasping for air—couldn't seem to breathe just right. He eased Target closer and put his left foot on the rock he'd been seated against. It was about two feet high. Facing Target's side, he grabbed the saddle horn and pulling with his arm while pushing with his left leg managed to mount. Spurring Target around, he headed south.

It wasn't much after daylight when he heard the first shot and then a distant call. At first he thought it might be the bushwhackers coming back, but then he recognized Monty's voice. Ballard pulled his Winchester from its boot and laying it across the saddle sideways was able to lever a shell into the firing chamber. Holding it in the air he fired. Within minutes Monty and Bridges were at his side.

"What happened boss? We've been sick with worry, and looking at you it appears we had good reason. We knew last night when you didn't show that something was wrong, especially when Matt Owen and his riders came in and they hadn't seen you since you left their camp."

Ballard told them what had happened, and as he talked, he heard barking in the distance and the two dogs ran up herding the donkey. When he finished, he said, "Now, I've told my story, it's your turn. Where are the horses, and what's this about Matt Owen?"

"Well, Owen and his crew showed up last night about midnight. Indians had stolen about sixty head of their horses and Mr. Chisum remembered you had ten to sell and sent Matt to pick them up. We didn't know how much you wanted, but he left $600 in gold and said if it wasn't right, you could collect the balance when they got back from Kansas."

Ballard's heart jumped. Maybe he had enough to save the ranch. Reaching in his saddlebag, he pulled out the sock, handed it to Bridges, and asked him to count its contents.

"Twelve hundred dollars, Boss. I get $1,200," he said. Ballard's hopes faded. Twelve hundred plus the $600 for the horses, or a total of $1800. Still short $200, close but not close enough. Chester Roberts wanted the ranch. He wouldn't take part payment, and he made it clear he wouldn't make a loan. It might as well have been a million short as $200.

Monty scratched his chin and said, "Guess there's no reason to be in a rush to get back to Three Forks?"

"No, there's nothing we can do. The ranch is lost."

"Well, since we're not in a hurry, let Bridges look at your wounds while he whips us up some breakfast. What you say?"

Ballard agreed some grub probably wouldn't hurt. They moved over into a grove of trees and set up camp. Bridges took Ballard's makeshift bandages off, washed his wounds again, applied some horse liniment which burned like hell, and rebandaged him with strips of blanket. In the meantime, Monty had built a small fire and filled the coffee pot with water from a nearby stream, and Ballard saw him reach into the pack for coffee.

David Thomasson

"What the heck," Monty exclaimed as he dropped something he was trying to pull out of the pack. Then in a puzzled voice, "Say, how come this coffee is so heavy?"

Ballard stood up so fast he almost fainted, and said, "Because there's $700 in gold in it and that means we've got $2500—more than enough to save the ranch!"

Ballard had forgotten all about finding the gold in the bushwhacker's pack. It was a sort of justice: Their money would be used to replace money stolen by their friends. "Monty, saddle up. You and I've got a ride to make." It was ten in the morning of the twenty-ninth day and they were about sixty miles from Three Forks.

"Boss, let Bridges and me go. You're not up to such a ride."

"No, I've got to be there in case something goes wrong. I can't take the risk of losing the ranch. Bridges can take the donkey and dogs back to the ranch. You can come along and keep an eye on me to make sure I get to Three Forks."

Neither said anything, although Ballard could tell they didn't like the plan much.

From the very beginning, the ride was painful as the bandages rubbed on Ballard's open wounds. Target was a smooth riding horse, as smooth as there was in the world, but smooth or not, a certain amount of movement occurs when you ride a horse cross country. Within an hour, the pain settled into a constant agony. From time-to-time, Ballard felt blood run down his side, and soon it soaked his shirt. Blood was also trickling from around his headband over his eyebrow into his left eye. He had to hold the reins with his right hand so he had no way to get the blood out of his eye. Mixing with the trail dust it soon crusted all over the entire left side of his face and neck.

Much later Ballard felt himself falling, and at the last minute, Monty's hand caught his arm. Monty said, "Boss, we've got to stop. That's the third time you've almost fell and it won't do any good to save the ranch if you die doing it."

Ballard knew Monty was right so he replied, "Look for a place."

They rode down an embankment and found a little rocky bottom under some spreading cedar limbs. Ballard sat stonily in the saddle while Monty built a fire. Once he had it going, he sensed Ballard was too weak to dismount and he came over and reached up, putting his hands under Ballard's arms, and eased him down. After a cold biscuit with jerky and some coffee, Ballard felt slightly better.

"How far did we come?" he asked.

"I reckon at least thirty-five miles, with about twenty-five to do tomorrow."

Ballard nodded affirmative. Just about what he had guessed.

Ballard didn't speak again, and as the fire began to warm his aching body, he fell into a troubled sleep. Huge bears were chasing him, Indians were throwing lances, men without faces were shooting. He was on foot, running uphill on a piece of ground that had cracked out of the earth's crust and tilted up. Flames were coming up around its edges. He was exhausted from the chase, and as he began to slow down, he slid toward the flame-filled crack. His legs were heavy and he knew he couldn't run anymore and as he started to fall he screamed.

"Boss, Boss, you're having a nightmare. Wake up!"

Ballard opened his eyes. "What time is it?"

"I make it about four o'clock. Time to go," he said as he handed him a scalding hot cup of coffee.

The heat burned his mouth, throat, and stomach, but he gulped it down because it actually felt good compared to the agony of his wounds. In a way, it took his mind off the real hurt.

"Don't fix me any food," Ballard said, "I don't feel so hungry."

Monty looked at him but didn't ask the question on his mind because Ballard evidently felt as rocky as he looked. "Help me up, it's time to ride."

As he helped him into the saddle, Ballard felt his shoulder wound break loose and start to bleed again. "Now, tie my hands to the saddle horn and my feet under Targets belly."

"No boss, I won't do it."

"Monty, I'm weak. I might fall. If I fall I won't have the will to get up. Now, tie me on. We're going to Three Forks."

****

The clock on the front of Rancher's Bank said 2:13 when they rode down the main street. The few people about turned to stare. Ballard could feel blood pooling in his boots; his shirt, pants and saddle were caked with it.

They pulled to a stop in front of the Sheriff's Office. Sheriff Bosque watched soberly, leaning against the door jam, as Monty cut him loose. "Don't just stand there. Open a jail cell and turn the cover down on a bunk, Sheriff," Monty shouted.

The sheriff spun to carry out his orders as several hands lifted Ballard from the saddle and carried him to the waiting bunk.

"Monty, bring the gold and count out the I.O.U. money."

He got the gold from the saddlebags and counted out ten stacks of double eagles on the Sheriff's desk top.

"Sheriff, write me a receipt acknowledging payment in full and canceling the foreclosure notice."

He did so. Looking around, Ballard spotted Chester Roberts in the back of the crowd. He was scowling and his face was flushed with anger.

"Mr. Roberts, take this receipt and the extra $500 in that bag and put it in the bank vault."

Ballard knew by giving it to him in front of all these people, it would be safe. With this Ballard collapsed into the land of the bears, Indians, shooters, and burning cracks.

— Chapter Twenty —

Blood in His Boots

IT SEEMED ONLY MINUTES later when Ballard felt a cool rag on his forehead, opened his eyes, and saw the face of Linda Harrison.

"Well, if it isn't Rip Van Winkle, finally deciding to wake up."

Moving his head slightly, he saw the bars on the door of the cell. Linda saw him looking and said, "Yes, you're still at the jail. Doc said not to move you or you might die. The good news is you're not a prisoner."

Ballard felt a bandage around his head and looking down saw a fresh one on his shoulder. Neither wound hurt as much as when he passed out and he suspected he'd been out for some time. She poured him a drink of water from a milk-colored pitcher that was on a table by the bed, and after a drink, he asked, in a husky voice he scarcely recognized. "How long have I been out?"

"Well, Rip," she said with a twinkle in her eye, "I count fifteen days. Doc said you didn't have enough blood left to fuel a cat. He said most of yours was in your boots. He didn't think you'd last the first night. But he had me make some chicken broth and force it down your throat. He also said we had to keep you from overheating, so we've been putting wet rags on your forehead and washing your chest. After the second day, he said you had a slight chance to live, and after the first week, he said you'd probably live."

Now that Ballard looked closer at her, she looked tired, in fact, exhausted. There were circles under her eyes, the whites were bloodshot, and her face was puffy from lack of sleep. Before he could find out the reason, a sinking spell hit him and he drifted back to the land of dreams.

When Ballard woke again, he was hungry and took this as a good sign. It was dark outside, but there was a light on and bending his head around he recognized Monty asleep with his head on the Sheriff's desk. Tapping a tin cup on the bars brought Monty running.

"Damn, Boss, we never thought you'd make it. You've had a tough go. Linda practically saved your life all by herself. She was here twenty-four hours a day until you woke up yesterday, and then we practically had to fight her to get her home for some rest. The town women got all mad, her being a single woman, and you being sick and naked and they said, 'it's just not Christian.' Well, Linda just looked them right in the eyes and said, 'A dying man isn't indecent, only sick and helpless,' and then she gave them two minutes to clear out or so help her she would wear a broom out on their behinds. They flounced out of here in such a huff they haven't been back."

Monty walked back to the Sheriff's desk, grabbed the chair, brought it over, sat down and continued, "After the first week, she worked twice as hard. She read to you, she washed your hands and face, and she talked. Sometimes as she talked, she would lay her head on your bunk and I began to worry about her. She looked so tired. Doc told her she had to go home and sleep. She wouldn't. She said, 'You'll have to drag me from this cell and nail the front door shut. I'll never leave until he's dead or out of danger.'"

"Yesterday, after you woke up, Doc wouldn't take no for an answer. He told her if she didn't go home, he'd pour laudanum down her throat to knock her out. She could tell he meant it, so she finally agreed to go. Doc had me get a buckboard—he knew she was too exhausted to even walk three blocks to Molly's—and we put her on blankets in the back. She fell asleep lying there. When I got her home, I carried her in and Molly put her to bed. She's been asleep ever since. I only wish she loved me like she does you."

His last statement jarred Ballard. He looked at Monty to see if he was joking, but one look at his serious face and Ballard knew it was true. Picking up a tin cup, Ballard hurled it at Monty. He ducked and it bounced off the wall. "Why, you dumb ox, she cared for me because I was wounded. She doesn't love me. All you have to do is go act a fool and get shot to rags and she'll love you just as much. Now, shut up that nonsense and go get me some food."

Monty jumped out of the chair and went over to look out the front door of the jail.

Ballard wondered what he was doing, but in a moment he called out, "Hey, Harry, over here." Harry Lindner, the boy from the livery, walked in.

"Harry, will you sit here with the boss while I run over to the Frontier and get him a steak?"

"Monty, I don't need a nursemaid. You'll only be gone a few minutes."

"Not on your life, Boss. You never saw her eyes. Doc swore someone would be with you until she got back. I'm not going to cross her."

Ballard could see he wasn't going to get anywhere with this moon-eyed galoot so he meekly said, "O.K., but make it snappy. Harry probably hasn't got all night to waste."

Harry took a seat by the bed and said, "Target is in the stable. Monty brought him down. I've been graining and grooming him every day. He was a little gaunt when they brought him in, but he's really cleaned up fine. He's about pawed the stall floor out, ready to run. I'll work him out, if you want me to."

"No, son, he's a one-man horse. Let him out in the corral for an hour each day and he'll get his exercise."

"There's a lot of talk about you and Miss Linda. Mrs. Rooney says you'll have to get married, her spending the nights here alone with you and all."

Ballard's temper began to boil. Everyone in town was talking, even the teenage boys. She was almost a stranger and the town already had them married. Ballard started to sit up in the bed and the cover fell away from his naked chest. Harry looked at him and then away, not wanting to see a naked man. Ballard felt himself blushing furiously because both he and Harry realized Linda had been seeing the same thing and more, for over two weeks. Maybe what local people said had some merit. Certainly, Ballard was beholden to her for saving his life, and now, after ruining her reputation, it would be a sorry repayment to throw her over if she wanted him. But his thoughts turned to Virginia Murphy, her big dark eyes, her animal grace. What role did she play in his life? His skin flushed with sweat. He hadn't spoken more than a sentence or two to a woman in the last month and yet he had woman trouble.

Monty returned with the food and broke this train of thought for the time being. The next morning, bright and early, Sheriff Bosque showed up.

"Feel like talking about what happened?"

Actually, Ballard felt much better. Maybe it was the food. In any event, he told the story about the man at Chisum's camp and the ambush.

"After you were shot did you hear any names, or see any faces?" Bosque asked.

"No, I was unconscious the whole time and didn't see or hear a thing."

This, of course, wasn't the truth, but, number one, Ballard didn't want a killer looking for him before he was well, and the story couldn't get out if he didn't tell it; and, number two, he wanted to personally settle a score or two with Lanny Weitzel and his friends.

"How about horses, or brands, did you see any?"

"No, Sheriff, it was pitch dark. Didn't even see the two men I shot, but if you'll look for two wounded men or two fresh graves it might tell you something."

Ballard didn't tell him it would definitely be two graves, and they'd have the names Ike and Joe on the markers. He also didn't tell him about the three dead men in the bear cave. Better let sleeping dogs lie.

"So they bushwhacked you to steal the gold?"

"They were after the gold, no doubt, but it goes a lot deeper than that, Sheriff. Whoever had my uncle killed was trying to get his ranch, and they're still trying and they probably live at the Rockin M."

"You accusing Murphy because his men shot your uncle?"

"I'm not accusing anyone. Let's just say, as soon as I get up and around, I'm going to have a talk with Mr. Murphy."

"Sounds like a threat to me."

"Sheriff, don't confuse a threat with a fact." Smelling cigar smoke, Ballard took a shot in the dark. "Why not ask your friend Chester Roberts to come in where he can hear better?"

Roberts stepped through the door, pausing to knock the ashes from his cigar.

"Actually, I just walked over to talk to the sheriff about a personal matter and I didn't want to interrupt your conversation."

"Sure. On the other hand, maybe the sheriff mentioned he was going to question me and you came along to see if I knew anything. There's all kinds of ways to look at the same thing. Maybe you and the sheriff are friends, or business associates?"

Both were looking at the floor and Ballard knew his comments had struck home.

"And while you were at it, why didn't you invite your other friend?"

They both looked startled, but before they could reply, Linda came through the door in a rush.

****

Straight to the bunk she came and folded in her arms were washed and pressed pants and a new shirt.

"I cleaned these pants, but your shirt was a little the worse for wear, what with bullet holes and bloodstains, so I got you another one from Horan's. Now, if you gentlemen will excuse us so he can get dressed."

The two men walked out the door without a reply, although Roberts did tip his hat to Linda. Linda held the clothes out saying, "Doc came by the store and said you could get up and move around today if you felt like it."

He took the clothes but made no move to rise. She stood watching him with her hands on her hips.

Finally, she got the idea and said, "Oh, for goodness sakes, I've been caring for you for weeks and now suddenly you're modest."

"Yep, but I was unconscious and didn't know. Now I do, and I'm not moving until you're on the front porch with the door closed."

She went out, closing the door, but as she went she said, "you've got ten minutes. Then I'll be back and if you're not dressed, I'll have to do it."

Nine minutes later he was dressed except for his boots, and called her back in. "I can't find my boots."

"Yes, I know. I took them over to the saddle shop to be cleaned. I'll pick them up today."

"Now, stand up," she said, as she moved over to his right side. As he rose, she took his arm and put it around her shoulders. Lucky she did because his head spun, gray dots flashed in front of his eyes, and he almost fell.

"Hold on tight," she said, almost like she was talking to a bronc rider, and God knows he felt like one, with the floor buckling and pitching, but in a few minutes he felt better and she said, "Now, let's walk."

They walked around the inside of the jail for a few minutes and she took him back to the bunk. He felt weak as a kitten and beads of sweat were on his forehead.

"I'm going to get your boots, then I'll come back and we'll walk over to the Frontier for breakfast."

"Well, if you're bound and determined to get me out in public, at least go by Lindner's and tell Harry Lindner to bring my bedroll so I can shave."

It was only a few minutes after she left when Harry trotted up with Ballard's bedroll in one hand and a small mirror in the other.

"Thought you might need this lookin' glass," he said.

Harry started for the door and began whistling the wedding march and never saw the tin cup coming which Ballard bounced off his head to help him in his future selection of appropriate tunes.

There was a wash bowl with a pitcher of water on a small whiskey barrel by the bunk. Ballard propped the mirror in back of the bowl and poured the bowl half full. Getting his razor and soap out of the bedroll, he set about making himself presentable. After he got the stubble off, the face he saw in the mirror looked thin and haggard. Not having eaten solid food for over two weeks had lost him 10-15 pounds. The bandage on his head hid the wound, but he was sure it would leave a scar on a face which he thought was already kind of plain. As he considered all this, he heard a step behind him and turned his head to see Doc Rodgers.

"Ran into Linda and she said you were going to make your public debut, so I figured I'd better come over and give you a checkup and change your bandages."

Rodgers pulled a stool up and said, "If you'll face me, please."

Ballard already had his shirt off for shaving. Rodgers unwrapped the bandage from around his shoulder. The wound was red and angry and still a little purple. "Hmm, no infection and it looks a lot less bruised than last week."

He rubbed some salve on it that caused a mild burning sensation and rebandaged it with a clean cloth. Next, he unwound Ballard's head bandage. As soon as it was off, Ballard reached over and picked up the hand mirror and looked at his face.

"So you're worried about your handsome face, are you?" asked the doctor. Without waiting for a reply he went on, "I thought you might be, so the first night you were here, I sewed up the head wound as best I could and took the stitches out a couple of days ago. Of course, you'll always have some scar over your eyebrow."

"Doc, I'm going to move over to the Frontier today and start eating regular foods. Any advice?"

"Well, don't put any stress on your shoulder. It's healing nicely, but any force could break it open again. You should be able to take up a fairly normal life in a few days. As far as the head wound is concerned, as long as you don't get pitched off a bronc or let someone slug you, not much can happen to it."

Linda came back at this point, and asked, "How's our patient?"

"Appears he don't need me anymore with you around to give him tender loving care."

She blushed slightly but smiled under his careful scrutiny and said, "Do unto others." She handed Ballard his boots and said, "Doc, we're going to breakfast. Want to go?"

"No, child, I've had breakfast long ago and I've got to stop by Mrs. Rooney's. She had a gout flareup, she says, although I suspect she wants to know the gossip about you and our friend here."

Ballard busied himself slipping on the boots, pretending he didn't have the slightest idea what they were talking about. They all walked out of the jail together, but Doc turned up the street toward the residential area, while Ballard and Linda walked directly across to the Frontier and into the dining room. It was after ten and no one else was eating, a fact which was just fine with Ballard. The waitress came and took their order and stared at Ballard's bandages the whole time.

After she left, Linda said, "Tomorrow if you want, we'll go on a picnic but after that I'll only be able to come by to see you at night. I got a job at Horan's right after you and Monty brought me to town and Mr. Horan was kind enough to let me off to nurse you. And although he hasn't asked, I know he needs help. You're doing so well that I went by and told him I'd come back tomorrow."

Ballard looked at her, concerned he might have caused her additional financial hardship, but she saw the look and said, "Don't worry, several families heading west came through the other day and one of their wagons broke down and it couldn't be repaired. I sold them our old wagon for $250, and then sold the horses and harness to Lindner for $200. I've got $450 in the bank and a job that pays me enough to live on."

"Well, I've got more good news for you," Ballard said, and told her about the three men who stampeded the herd and about finding the gold and how he was sure these men were the ones who stole her $200 and he had it for her over at Rancher's Bank.

She said, "I've got all I need. I want you to take the money and use it until you can get the ranch back on its feet, and when that's done, you can give it back."

Ballard already owed her so much—but she was right. He needed to pay Monty and Bridges and his bill at the livery and Horan's, and now was no time for pride. Roberts had already made it clear he wouldn't make him a loan, so Ballard said, "If that's what you want, it's exactly what I'll do and I appreciate the loan."

After breakfast Ballard checked into the hotel and went up to his room to rest while Linda returned to Molly's. He slept till dark and went down to the dining room to eat. The first person he saw when he reached the entrance was Virginia Murphy, sitting alone, and he started to turn and leave, but she looked up and saw him and beckoned. He walked guiltily over with his head down and she said, "If I didn't know better, I'd say you were about to try to avoid me."

Ballard didn't deny it or say anything so she said, "What's the matter, cat got your tongue?"

He had mixed feelings. He was almost magnetically drawn to her but felt deep obligation to Linda and was repelled by what he knew about the Rockin M.

"No, the cat hasn't got my tongue. I don't think it's good for us to be seen together. Your dad and I are not friends and as soon as I'm better, we'll probably be even less so."

"My dad can take care of himself, but I think you're wrong about him. He may be tough, but he's fair and he'd never bushwhack anyone."

"So you've been talking to Sheriff Bosque."

"Yes. He said you suspected the source of your troubles was the Rockin M and you'd made threats about getting even."

"Look, all I said was I was coming out to talk to your dad, nothing more. It was no threat."

She regarded him closely for a few moments, her eyes looking deeply into his. "I want to believe you, I don't know why. For some reason, I think a lot about you, even though I hardly know you. The day I came into town and heard you'd been seriously wounded, I wanted to rush over and help, but I heard you were in capable hands. In fact, I heard they're so capable you're going to marry your nurse. Ever since I heard that, I've been depressed. I feel I've lost something, although I don't know how I could lose something I never had. Now, I look into your eyes and I feel even more confused. Local people say you should marry Linda, but what they say means little. Tell me, is it true, will you marry Linda?"

✳✳✳✳✳✳✳✳✳✳✳✳✳✳✳✳✳✳✳✳✳✳✳✳✳✳✳✳✳

Before Ballard could form an adequate answer in his mind, Plunk Murray came to the table and said, "Miss Murphy, your father says it's time to head back. He's waiting out front with the surrey."

For a moment she looked at Ballard's face as if trying to read his thoughts, then she rose and said, "Perhaps I already know the answer" and walked away with her head high like a wild mustang in a mountain meadow.

Plunk Murray stood for a second, and said, "I don't know what that's about, but you better become accustomed to those bandages if you do anything, anything at all, to hurt that girl," and he turned and followed her out.

Ballard didn't doubt Murray's words in the least, knowing he felt very protective toward her. No doubt Murray had heard talk around town. Trouble was, Ballard didn't know if he'd hurt her, or if he did, how, and if so, it was the last thing in the world he'd intended to do.

All that night Ballard twisted and turned. His mind repeated Virginia's question. Dawn rose on his storm-tossed bed with no resolution to the problem of being obligated to one woman and loving another.

Noon that day found Ballard and Linda in the livery buckboard on the way to a picnic. At first, it seemed she couldn't make up her mind where to have the picnic. She drove south and then turned around and headed north. The result was that they drove through town twice and every tongue and eye in town was either wagging or blinking. They were local headline news, no doubt about it. Ballard had resolved it couldn't go on this way and he'd confront her with the truth, but each wave to Mrs. Johnson, hello to Mrs. Rooney, and how you do to Mrs. Lindner melted his resolve, and by the time they arrived at a shady grove of trees overlooking a flowing stream, he felt helpless. They were already notorious, and this picnic didn't help the situation. Linda had been chatting while Ballard, on the other hand, had been silent.

Finally, after they had the blanket spread and were eating, she said, "Why so quiet? You've hardly spoken ten words today."

"Oh, I've got a lot on my mind. I'm anxious to get out to the ranch and get to work."

"But Monty and Bridges can handle the ranch, and you need to be here in town where you can see the doctor."

"Maybe so, but people are beginning to talk. Seems they don't know the difference between nursing and courting."

She looked at him and said, "There's nothing wrong with two eligible people courting, and I want you to know that's exactly what I'm doing. I've fallen in love with you and I want to marry you."

Ballard's worst fears were realized. He put his two fingers over her lips and said, "Don't say things you might regret later, not until you're completely sure. You haven't known me long enough to know what you feel."

She was shaking her head from side-to-side and trying to speak, but he didn't take his finger down.

"Listen to me. Soon, I'm going back to the ranch. In six weeks, we have the Old Timers' Dance. I'll come in and we'll go to the dance and decide. If you still want me, we'll set the date."

For a moment, she looked upset or disappointed, an expression that Ballard couldn't quite read, but then she seemed to glance over his shoulder and suddenly brushed aside his hand and leaped across the blanket, throwing her arms around his neck and kissing him on the lips. As she released him, he heard horses hooves and looking around saw Red Murphy and Plunk Murray riding by on the road. The men didn't acknowledge them, but Ballard could tell from their stiff bearing they had seen what had just been done.

As Ballard looked at Linda, he noticed a hardness about her eyes and mouth he'd never seen before. Why had she done it? Was she overcome by emotion? It seemed so, but it also seemed she saw Murphy behind him and staged the whole thing. But if so, why? To make her mark on him? To warn Virginia away? On the other hand, she might just be a scheming woman and if so, she knew him well enough to weave a trap of honor and obligation from which he could not escape.

No matter the answer. Unless something happened in the next six weeks, his mouth, if not his heart, had bound him to marry Linda.

— Chapter Twenty-One —

Framed for Murder

BUD HARDIN CROSSED THE street from the Silver Spur and walked into the lobby of the Rancher's Bank. He looked carefully around, making sure no customers were there, and entered the half glass door with the name "Chester Roberts, President" on it.

Linda Harrison, seated in a chair across from Roberts, said, "I'm glad you're here. It didn't work out the way we planned. I can't get Ballard to do what we want, at least, not in time. The railroad buyer will be here in three weeks. We've got to have the ranch by then. Once the railroad man comes to town, the lid will be off and we won't be able to buy or steal land around here. Somehow we've got to get rid of him and still get title to the land."

Roberts interrupted, "Maybe we can use the same trick we used on Ben. Once he's dead, we'll produce the I.O.U. and foreclose on the ranch."

"Yep," Hardin replied. "But he may not be as easy to kill as Ben. Ben didn't even carry a gun. Lanny had to put one in his hand after he was dead."

Linda continued, "No matter whether he's tough or not, it's got to be done. So, we lose three, four, or even a dozen men. In the end, we'll get him. We've also got to deal with Red Murphy. If Murphy and Ballard die, we'll have the Rockin M, the Circle B, and the whole basin sewed up."

"What about Virginia?" Roberts asked.

"Don't worry about her. This is what we're going to do. I think we can kill two birds with one shot, so to speak."

Once the directions were given, Linda stepped from the office and left the bank. Somewhat later, Bud Hardin left by the side door.

✶✶✶✶✶✶✶✶✶✶✶✶✶✶✶✶✶✶✶✶✶✶✶✶✶✶✶✶✶

Ballard's last three days in town passed without a problem. Linda was working, and other than the doctor checking the wounds every day, he didn't talk to anybody. By Friday he was restless and ready to go, and the doctor reluctantly said he could. Bridges had come into town for supplies and Ballard decided to ride back with him in the wagon.

As the supplies were being loading at Horan's dock, Bud Hardin and Red Murphy rode up. Murphy said, "Ballard, there's lots of things I'll tolerate, but one thing I won't is someone trifling with my daughter's affections. It's my understanding you and Linda Harrison are going to get married, and from what I've seen recently, it'll come none too soon to protect her reputation."

Ballard blushed, remembering Linda kissing him as Murphy rode by.

"And yet," he went on, "I heard my daughter crying in the night and when I ask why, she won't say. Plunk Murray thinks it has something to do with you."

Murphy looked at Ballard, wanting an answer, but Ballard had none. Murphy's words were true to the mark. Nothing Ballard could say would help, and anything he said would cause trouble. In his place Ballard would have thought the same thing. Ballard's silence seemed to enrage Murphy and he wheeled and rode away.

Bud Hardin didn't leave with him. He said, "Ballard, Mr. Murphy thinks it would be better for you to pack up and leave. He's willing to buy whatever interest you have in your uncle's ranch. He told me to offer you $15,000 provided you take it and leave without speaking to his daughter. He's at the bank now if you'll take the deal."

The offer was more than fair, but it rankled Ballard that they were trying to buy him off. He looked at Hardin and said, "The Rockin M is no friend of mine, and if my ranch was for sale, Murphy is the last person I'd sell it to."

Hardin didn't look surprised. In fact, he looked kind of content as he said, "Its your funeral," and rode off toward the bank.

Maybe he should have sold. It might have saved a lot of trouble. But Ballard was a stubborn man and had he left, no one would have paid for his uncle's death or the things that had happened to Ballard himself. The longer he held on, the more likely he was to find out who did it. Murphy seemed to be the logical suspect, but considering he was Virginia's father, Ballard had trouble believing he was a low-life, murdering thief.

After the wagon was loaded, Ballard went in and signed the bill and Horan handed him the receipt. Again, it looked familiar and Ballard reached in his pocket and pulled out the receipt he had found on Jeffers. They weren't the same, but Ballard knew he'd seen a similar receipt somewhere. As Ballard and Bridges walked out, they noticed Murphy riding by alone, evidently heading home. This might be Ballard's chance to talk to Murphy, man-to-man. *I might be able to get the trouble straightened out,* he thought.

Turning to Bridges, he said, "I've changed my mind. I'm going to ride Target out to the ranch. I'll meet you when you get in."

Bridges had seen the direction of Ballard's glance and as Murphy disappeared, he said, "Be careful, Boss, he's got a hot temper."

"Don't worry. I just want to talk to him."

Heading for the livery, Ballard almost ran over Horan and realized he had overheard their conversation, but at the time didn't think anything about it. Harry wasn't around the livery and neither was Ballard's saddle. He waited, but Harry didn't come back for about ten minutes.

"Sorry, I had to deliver Mrs. Rooney's hack. She going visiting."

"Where's my gear?"

"The saddle was all blood-stained and was dry and cracking so I took it over to the saddle shop to be conditioned."

Harry ran across the street and returned with Ballard's saddle, but by the time he paid and rode out, Murphy had a 30-minute head start. Target was ready to run and he let him open up.

When Ballard got to the turn between the Circle B and Rockin M, he stopped. It was one thing to talk to Murphy on open range and quite another to follow him onto his own land. He might shoot Ballard on sight and the law would be on his side. Ballard glanced ahead at the horse's tracks, which were plain for the following. Murphy was evidently only a few minutes ahead. He hesitated for a moment and realizing the danger, turned toward the Circle B, deciding their talk would have to wait for another time.

When Ballard got to the ranch, no one was there, but an hour later, Bridges pulled in and unloaded the supplies. About dark, Monty rode in from checking the ranch for cattle and horses missed in the roundup.

"I make it about sixty cattle and several horses still around, but there's a herd of wild mustangs to the west we could also catch and break."

All in all, it was good news, a lot better than no ranch, no cattle. So, for the first time in weeks, Ballard was at home and had a future to look forward to; that night he slept soundly.

The next morning they were eating breakfast when they heard riders approaching. As Ballard started for the front, he picked up his Winchester from the kitchen corner and walked out on the porch just as Sheriff Bosque, Bud Hardin, Ed Seiker, and several other riders, some from the Rockin M, some from town, stopped at the front hitch rail.

"What happened, someone rob the bank?" Ballard asked. He knew it had to be something big to get this kind of posse out.

"No, the bank wasn't robbed. Red Murphy was shot." This surprised Ballard and he didn't know what to say.

"Ballard, put your rifle down," the sheriff said as he dismounted, and while his body was shielded by his horse drew his pistol and pointed it at Ballard's face. "Why?" Ballard said, with the rifle still in the crook of his arm.

"Because all the evidence says you're the murderer. You shot Murphy."

Murphy was dead, they believed he did it, and here he stood with a rifle that didn't even have a shell in the firing chamber. What a fool. Before he could lever a shell in, he'd be shot down.

As Ballard hesitated, he heard. "Drop the gun, Ballard" from behind him and looking over his shoulder saw Lanny Weitzel with a pistol in his hand. Evidently, Weitzel had ridden up on the opposite side of the house and crept around behind him. Ballard was filling up with anger and seeing Weitzel's smirking face made him feel reckless.

"Well, if it isn't Lanny the Weasel. How's Joe and Ike? Haven't seen them around for awhile."

Weitzel's eyes glittered like a cornered rattlesnake, and Ballard knew he got the message.

Ballard could see Weitzel's finger beginning to tighten on the trigger, so saying, "O.K., I give up," he tossed his rifle sideways toward him. As Weitzel reached to catch it with his empty hand, Ballard stepped inside his pistol and hit him a vicious blow to the mouth. Weitzel's head bounced off the wall and he fell in a heap. Ballard kicked the gun from Weitzel's fist, raised his hands, and turned to face the posse.

The Sheriff dismounted and handcuffed Ballard around a porch support post. Monty and Bridges had come out of the house and were standing quietly behind him.

The Sheriff looked at them and said, "One of you saddle his horse."

Monty waited until Ballard nodded and then went to the corral, saddling Target and his own horse, and returned leading both.

The sheriff looked at Monty and said, "Where do you think you're going?"

"For a ride."

"Well, it's not going to be with us."

"Never said it was, but is there any reason you wouldn't want another person along? Haven't got anything planned you don't want me to see, have you?"

"Think what you like, but I've never lost a prisoner yet and this one is going to stand trial, and you're not riding with us."

Monty said, "Bridges, hand me my Winchester."

As Bridges returned from the kitchen with the rifle, Hardin and the Sheriff and several others drew their pistols and covered Monty. Bridges handed him the rifle and he turned casually toward the barn. Raising the rifle to his shoulder, he fired three shots as rapidly as he could crank the lever. It was a good three hundred yards to the barn and each shot brought a clank from the old tin rooster on its roof. When the smoke cleared, the rooster was spinning wildly and all three of its tail feathers were missing. Bosque looked puzzled. Monty never said another word, just deliberately reloaded and slid the rifle into his saddle boot.

Finally, the Sheriff shrugged and said, "Let's ride." He unlocked Ballard from the post, let him mount, and then cuffed his wrists back together.

As soon as they left the yard, it started. First Seiker, "Let's string him up. He don't deserve no trial."

Then Hardin, "Anybody who's shot a man in the back needs hanging. What about it, Sheriff?"

Bosque didn't say anything, but by his silence, he was acquiescing. He looked around as if concerned that someone might see what was going to happen, Ballard could guess the plan—incite the honest men, then string him up. His chances of making it to town were slim, but suddenly the sheriff held up his hand for everyone to stop. Looking back, they could see Monty stopped on a ridge some 200 yards behind. His rifle could be clearly seen in his hand with its butt propped on one leg and its barrel in the air. The message was clear: if Ballard didn't make it to town neither would a lot of other people. If Monty could clip tin feathers off a spinning rooster at 300 yards, he'd have no trouble with a man at 200. The rest of the way to town the men rode in silence.

As Bosque locked Ballard in the cell, he said, "Judge Coulter will be through in two weeks. Your trial will be then."

Bosque walked out, leaving Hardin standing in front of the cell.

"You should have sold and left. You'll never make it till the trial. You're a walking dead man."

"What's the matter, Bud? Afraid they'll ask too many questions and find out about Joe and Ike and who's the real rotten meat at the Rockin M?"

"You think you know it all, huh? If you really knew, it'd knock your socks off," Hardin said as he walked away. What did he mean? Who was involved? Red Murphy was dead and it couldn't be Virginia. One thing was sure—Ballard couldn't find out if he was dead and every minute he stayed in this jail was another nail in his coffin. He broke out of his thinking as he heard a small rock hit the window at the back of the cell. He looked out the window and saw Monty.

"What can I do to help, Boss? All the Rockin M's over at the Silver Spur drinking and it looks like a hanging is in the air."

As Ballard felt the iron bars, it came to him. "Go get Target and tell the Sheriff you're taking him to the livery. Take him over there and get him some grain and a good rubdown. Just after dark, saddle him and bring him to the hotel shed across the alley behind you. Put his reins over the saddle horn, your Winchester in the boot, and your cartridge belt and pistol over the horn. Then go over to the Silver Spur and stay in plain sight until ten o'clock and then start a fight. The sheriff will hear the ruckus and come over to see what it's all about. Leave the rest to me. If everything goes O.K., meet me with supplies at the hidden valley two days from now. If I don't show, leave the supplies on top of the old stone wall and head back to the ranch. You and Bridges will have to watch the ranch. They might try to burn us out. Don't leave there until you hear from me. Got it?"

Monty nodded yes. "Well, beat it before someone spots you."

****

As Ballard sat waiting for night, the front door opened and in walked Virginia Murphy. He could see she had been crying. Her eyes were red and the lids a little puffy. She stopped a good two yards from the cell, almost like she was afraid of catching some contagious disease. The look in her eyes was mixed hurt, disappointment, anger, and hate. "How could you? You said, you only wanted to talk to Dad and you shot him in the back.

To think I may have even helped. I told him you were honest and he had misjudged you. How could I have been so wrong?"

"You weren't, Virginia. I swear you weren't. I didn't kill him. I didn't even see him on the way home."

"I'd like to believe you, Adam, but Horan told the Sheriff you left his store to catch my dad. The sheriff followed your tracks to where he was shot and found a pistol that several people have identified as yours. In addition, you've told everyone who'd listen that you were going to have a heart-to-heart talk with my dad."

"Virginia, I know how it looks and how it sounds, but it's just not true. I lost that pistol when I was shot. Whoever shot me must have found it and used it to shoot your dad. And besides, why would I leave my pistol where it could be found? The evidence is circumstantial. It wouldn't hold up under close scrutiny. If I was out of here, I could prove it."

She seemed to be weakening. Most of the distrust was leaving her eyes, when Linda walked through the door. Ballard's hands were on the bars and Linda walked right to the cell and put her hands on his. "Sweetheart," she said, "Murphy only got what he deserved after what he did to you. The court will say it was self-defense." And she stared at Virginia with pure hate in her eyes.

Virginia turned and Ballard said, "Virginia, wait."

She replied, "No, she's partly right. The court will decide, but I think it'll be 'guilty of murder.'"

With this she left.

"Linda, there's something I've been wondering about. How did Murphy know we might get married? You and I were the only ones who knew. How did he find out?"

"Well, I don't know. I did tell Molly and maybe she told someone. I was so excited, I couldn't keep it a complete secret."

She's the only one you told?"

"Yes, the only one." It didn't seem right. Molly was close-mouthed and she certainly didn't run with the Rockin M crowd, but it could have happened and it would be hard to prove one way or the other.

Linda said, "I think you'll get a fair trial. You are going to stand trial, aren't you?"

For some unexplained reason Ballard didn't want to tell her about his escape plan, so he just shrugged his shoulders and said, "What choice do I have? No chance of breaking out of here."

She seemed relieved and somehow Ballard knew she wanted him right here until the trial. Did this mean she thought he would win, that he was innocent, that the evidence was really on his side . . . or was it that she wanted him hung? If so, why?

— Chapter Twenty-Two —

Whistling Up Target

SHORTLY AFTER DARK, BALLARD heard a horse being led into the hotel shed next door. The sheriff was at his desk, but the noise wasn't loud enough for him to hear. Everything was now in place. All Ballard had to do was wait.

The evening seemed endless, the hands on the clock above the sheriff's desk moved so slow. Ballard lay on his back and counted to a thousand and turned and looked at the clock.

Five minutes had passed. He must have misread the clock. It was impossible to count to a thousand in only five minutes. He faced the ceiling again and counted slower and looked again. Six minutes had passed.

Finally, Ballard said, "Sheriff what time is it?"

"Are you blind?" he said, pointing at the clock.

"No, but that clock is broken, isn't it?"

He laughed a cruel laugh. "No, time slows down when you're in jail, but once they sentence you to hang, those hands just fly around the numbers."

By nine o'clock, the noise level at the Silver Spur had increased and the crowd seemed to be getting rowdy. Ballard began to worry they might not wait till after ten o'clock to charge the jail. The sheriff also heard the increasing noise, and rising to his feet said, "I better go make my rounds."

It came to Ballard like a clap of thunder. The sheriff was planning to be gone when the mob came. No finger of suspicion could be pointed at him if he wasn't here.

"Sheriff, that crowd from the Silver Spur could get out of hand. Why don't you stay here."

"They won't bother you. I've got to make sure all the doors are locked, and Rob Taylor has been after me to check his place. He's been missing some cattle."

"But sheriff, his place is ten miles south."

"What's the matter Ballard? You're squealing like a pig under a gate."

The sheriff's eyes gleamed like agate, a smiling sneer on his face as he opened the door and said, "We'll see you later, Ballard," and closed the door.

Ballard heard him walk along the boardwalk and rattle a couple of doorknobs and then return and mount his horse and ride south. The sheriff had turned out the lamp as he left and Ballard couldn't see the clock in the pitch black of the jail's interior, but he estimated it to be 9:30. Listening to the growling sound across the street, he decided not to wait any longer.

Ballard put his fingers to his lips and whistled, not as loud as he could, but loud enough to bring Target trotting to the window. It was as dark outside as in, and black as Target was, Ballard couldn't see him, but he could certainly feel his big body. Talking softly, he eased the horse sideways and took the belt and pistol from the saddle horn and put them on. Next, he untied the lariat and secured one end to the saddle horn and the other around the base of the right hand window bar. Earlier when Ballard was talking to Monty, he had felt these bars move. They were in holes, which appeared to be about a foot deep, surrounded by rocks and mortar. "Backup, Target, backup, big boy." Target obediently tightened the slack out of the rope. "Hold Target, hold 'em."

Target was trained to hold cattle. Once they were roped, he knew to keep the rope tight so they couldn't get up. Reaching out the window, Ballard felt the rope tight as a guitar string. Putting both hands on it, Ballard yanked, at the same time saying "Hold em, steady boy," Feeling the yank, Target reacted the same way he would when a longhorn tried to get up by throwing his entire weight in opposition. As he did this, Ballard pushed on the bottom of the bar, and it popped out of its socket. Ballard caught it as it slid out of the top hole. It was a good five feet long and heavy. He stood it in the corner of the cell. As they repeated the procedure on the second bar, Ballard heard the noise from the saloon reach a new pitch and recognized the sound of a fight. He couldn't see the clock, but he knew it must be ten o'clock. He had to remove one more bar and only hoped the fight would last until he could. As the rope tightened on the last bar, Ballard heard the mob burst from the saloon doors across the street. He yelled at Target and heard the bar pop out just as the front door slammed open. He knew he'd never have time to squeeze through the window, so catching the falling bar he whirled to face the cell door. All he could see was a mass of shadows crowded into the dark hall. They couldn't see him at all in the gloom of the cell, they were swaying drunkenly calling his name.

"Ballard, we've got a necktie for you."

"Time to go for a short trip with a quick stop." This brought gales of drunken laughter.

"Someone get the key off the wall."

Bile rose in Ballard's throat. They were just a bunch of murderers. They deserved no more than they were trying to give. He waited no longer. Raising the iron bar to eye level Ballard thrust it viciously between the front bars of the cell. He felt it strike hard, heard the sickening crunch of bones and the scream of pain that followed. Pulling it back he thrust again, waist high. More screams this time—of terror as well as pain. Again, but this time at knee level. By this time, a general panic had set in and people were scrambling over each other's backs to escape. Muffled shots rang out as those on the bottom shot at the ones who were trampling them. In a few seconds, it was all over and the crowd had fled out the front door, leaving those dead or too crippled to notice him as he quietly slipped through the window, mounted Target, and rode slowly down the alley behind Shorty's and out of town.

****

Adam Ballard's pursuers probably thought he'd head north into the wild area near the ranch and that's exactly what he wanted them to think. Just north of town, the road rose up out of the river canyon through a rocky shelf and that's as far north as he went. Up to this point, his tracks were obscured by the traffic on this, the main road, and he would leave none on the rock.

He was just north of the confluence of the Llano River and its two branches, the North and South Llano. He doubled back and headed down the South Llano. Riding on the rock until dawn, Ballard estimated he had covered twenty-five miles. By now, the river had swung due west. He was now on the edge of the great empty land, the land of the Apache, coyote, and scorpion. His companions would be the rattler, the cactus, and the chaparral. Not many civilized people visited this area. Around the river, the land was lightly covered with buffalo grass, and tilted gradually to the north. This was a dry semi arid region some would call a desert.

Ballard filled his canteen and washed his face and body. Few white men knew the area he was going into and the water was going to be sparse so he took advantage of the opportunity he had. As he rode away from the river, from horizon-to-horizon, there was a sea of mesquite, prickly pear, agarita, and cholla. In places, red earth thrust through the green. Some of the cactus had large yellow flowers, and made a dangerous contrast—a 100 thorns waited for the hand of the person who harvested these beauties.

He fought his way through the heavy brush eventually coming to the fork of two small canyons and took the one on the left, hoping to rise above the thick growth. This presently brought him to an open ridge, where he reined up to blow Target. Behind and below, to the south and east, the wide expanse of the river basin opened. The flat was spotted by the shadows of the scattered clouds overhead. A buzzard glided overhead, otherwise, the land seemed devoid of life.

He picked his way north for a couple of hours, the river flats gradually dissolving into the fawn limestone of the plateau. Again, he stopped to blow Target and looked a second time over his backtrail. This time his scrutiny was rewarded because there was a plume of dust, the kind horsemen make.

They were at least three hours behind him. The best thing to do was to cover his tracks while he had time. On his right was a patch of solid rock. He rode on the rock for a few hundred yards then doubled back, cutting his own trail. Circling, he repeated this innumerable times, steadily working his way north. After an hour he came upon the trail of a band of mustangs drifting westward. Dismounting while still on solid rock, he unrolled his bedroll and cut four strips off his blanket, and with some rawhide string from his saddle, tied them on Target's hooves so he had cloth boots. Then, he headed westward in the trail left by the wild horses. His tracks would now blend with their unshod hooves.

Riding this way for some forty-five minutes, he came to the banks of a shallow stream where the horses had watered. He rode into the ankle-deep water, removed the cloth boots, put them in his saddlebags, and turned north with the stream, carefully staying in the water and on the rock so as to leave no sign.

Toward sundown, he came to a spring that welled out of a limestone outcropping rising some 30 feet above the surrounding land. The water from the spring flowed across the ground for a 100 or so feet into the stream bed. The surrounding area was green with grass and nearby there was a shallow cave. He was tired and Target was spent and tomorrow would likely bring even more of the same, so he decided to halt for the night.

After stripping the saddle, he took Target to the spring for a drink and rubbed him down with clumps of bunch grass and put him on a picket rope. He built a small almost smokeless fire from dried sticks and made some coffee, drinking it with some jerky. It was dusk as he finished eating, and he scooped dirt onto the fire and then carried water from the spring and poured it on top of the dirt. He didn't want to risk the fire or its glow being seen in the gathering gloom.

Just before dark, he took his blanket and climbed to the top of the limestone outcrop. The blanket he put around his shoulders against the Hill Country night's chill. It wasn't unusual in the early spring for daytime temperatures to be in the seventies and to drop forty degrees almost as soon as the sun went down. As the last of the sunlight faded, he could see to the south the twinkle of a campfire. So, just as he'd imagined, they were still there, about two hours behind. Dawn found Ballard on a rising trail. As he left them, he again tied Target's cloth boots on, hoping anyone coming on the tracks would think they were those of a stray mustang. After riding for an hour he dismounted, led Target onto the rock, and removed his boots. Taking the reins, he began to pick his way on foot to the top of the mesa. Birds were whistling in the brush and a pair of red squirrels scolded at him as he passed. The top of the mesa was covered with cedar and as he reached the crest, a small herd of deer trotted off to the west, their white flags flashing as they disappeared. The land now, instead of being flat, was rising toward a high point that appeared to be a mile or two to the north. The cedar was so thick man and horse had to squeeze between the trees with the branches brushing both sides.

Eventually, he came to the high point, and he could see far down his back trail. The plume of dust was still there and seemed to be headed directly for him. Better keep moving, he thought. Remounting, he kicked Target in the ribs and headed across the top of the mesa west. The farther west he went, the dryer and dustier it got. Dust settled on his face and hat and he felt his neck growing raw from the chafing of his collar. The cedar had thinned out and in the distance, he could see a mirage on the horizon, but the heat waves were moving in closer, blotting out the distance, leaving only the oppressive shimmering dust. The country was increasingly broken, and he entered a sea of devil's claw, cholla, and prickly pear.

Hours later, both Ballard and Target were utterly exhausted when mounting a small rise, amid a continuing jungle of thorns and spikes,

Ballard spotted a small valley—just a pocket in the surrounding desert. It was almost sundown and even though there was no water in the valley, there was a little grass. Stripping the saddle off, Ballard put Target on a picket rope. From his canteen, he poured about half the remaining water into his hat. Target drank it greedily and licked the inside. Ballard took a small sip of water and held it in his mouth, letting it trickle down his throat. Shaking the canteen, he guessed it contained no more than four or five ounces. It wasn't much but it'd have to do. They'd need to find water no later than tomorrow night.

Ballard stripped his remaining gear from the horse, got his bedroll, spread the groundsheet with the blanket on top, and lay back. A whippoorwill was calling and in the distance, Ballard could hear a mother coyote teaching her pack of young to sing. A million stars twinkled overhead and he could hear Target pulling and chewing the clumps of grass nearby. No man could have asked for a more peaceful setting. The only thing keeping him awake was the chewing he was doing on the jerky and as soon as he finished he fell into a deep sleep.

Ballard woke with a start in predawn blackness. Bad men were a'coming. Maybe they knew of this place, although it wasn't likely because it didn't have any water and they'd have no reason to come here if there were other places with both grass and water.

Nonetheless, even if they didn't know of this particular place, they did know the surrounding terrain and probably could guess where he'd have to go to get water. Which meant he not only had to be concerned about his back trail, but also about being ambushed by those who had cut across and were waiting in front. Dew was heavy on his saddle and groundsheet and he soaked it up in his bandana and wiped Target's mouth out, squeezing what moisture he could onto his lips. Saddling up, he mounted and sat quietly chewing jerky until he could discern the surrounding land features. Kicking Target in the ribs, he headed out.

About midmorning, he saw a movement in the distance. Holding his hand to shade his eyes from the sun, he made out a blacktail deer walking over some small mounds ahead. In the past few miles, he had also noticed bees flying in the same general direction and now noticed the tracks of a packrat paralleling the same route. All this evidence could indicate there was water somewhere not too far ahead and he certainly hoped so because the sun was already blazing.

Some twenty minutes later, he mounted a small hill amid a thick forest of prickly pear and looked into a ravine. There was a startling and beautiful sight—water, not just a little water but a large, clear blue pool of water in a limestone bowl of rocks. Shading the pool were cottonwood and willow trees and near the edge was the sign of old camp fires.

Target strained at the reins, but Ballard held back. Something seemed wrong. Where was the deer? It had been just ahead of him, it should have been still drinking. Something must have frightened it. Now, there are things in the desert that frighten deer, like mountain lions, or wolves, but he saw no sign of either. Target stomped his feet impatiently and he was right, they had no choice, they had to have water. Pulling his Winchester from its boot and checking to make sure his pistol was loose in its holster, he released the reins and Target trotted toward the water.

****

Target was drinking and Ballard was looking around, with his rifle cocked and ready for anything. Suddenly Target's head came up and he looked directly at a plum thicket about 75 feet away against a rock bank. A tawny-colored shape suddenly burst out of the ticket and sped up and over the rocks out of sight.

"Easy boy," Ballard said as Target snorted and danced around at the sight of the cougar. The big cat explained the absence of the deer.

Target finished drinking. Ballard dismounted, washed his face, refilled his canteen, and turned back to the desert again. He hadn't ridden two miles when looking up a rise at the entrance to a small valley, he saw the sun reflecting off a rifle barrel and dove from his saddle behind a patch of prickly pear.

— Chapter Twenty-Three —

Burning Bridges

FRANK BRIDGES FELT THE rope settle around his body and instantly dove toward his rifle. He had left it leaning against the barn as he saddled his horse and now cursed himself for being so careless. I should have checked around the barn before I put it down, he mumbled under his breath. Just as his hand was about to close on its barrel, the rope pulled his arms against his sides and he was yanked away from the rifle. Before he could see who had him, a feedsack was pulled over his head and strong hands gripped his arms. Blindly he was dragged into the corral.

"Bring him over here," he heard in hushed tones as he was hauled up against the snubbing post in the center of the corral. Forced to kneel, he was bound tightly with his body on one side of the post and his hands and feet behind his back on the other. A rope was pulled tight around his throat so he could not turn his head without scraping his neck and couldn't lean forward without gagging. Several horses were led into the corral and they had one thing in common—they all smelled of kerosene. He heard the riders unwrapping their bedrolls and guessed they had kerosene-soaked rags in their slickers. Several of the men walked away and it wasn't long before he smelled oily smoke coming from the direction of the house. Soon, the popping and crackling of burning wood verified his suspicions. They had fired the house. He struggled against his ropes in helpless fury. Steps approached and a voice he didn't recognize at the time said, "It's going to get hot here pretty quick. I could move you. Where's your partner?"

They wanted to know where Monty was. Well, Monty was gone to deliver the supplies to the hidden valley, but Frank wasn't about to tell them, so he merely shook his head no. His nod was followed immediately by a stunning blow that hammered his head against the post, and a knee to this ribs that drove the wind from his body. Despite the pain, his resolve wasn't dented. Having been tortured by Indians once and having lived in frontier danger all his life, he wasn't about to be stampeded by a bunch of tinhorn house-burners.

His thoughts were interrupted by a second and a third blow that exploded the world into blackness. When he awoke coughing and choking against the rope, he realized he had been pistol whipped. He could feel warm liquid running over his forehead under the sack and knew it was his blood. He could scarcely breathe because of the rope.

"Last chance, you stubborn old coot, where's your partner?" He didn't even bother to nod. "Let the old idiot fry," followed by a cruel laugh he'd never forget, and only moments later a rifle butt cracked into his head sending him back to the land of the golden pinwheels and exploding suns.

He was awakened later by the smell of smoke and by oppressive heat. His whole body was searing and the smoke was not from wood burning but from the cloth over his face smoldering. The heat from the burning barn was so intense it was igniting the feed sack. Despite his dizziness, he desperately crawled around the post, putting it between him and the fire. This was only a temporary solution because immediately he felt the bare skin on his hands begin to burn and blister. Yanking his feet toward the post brought his boot tops into his hands. Pulling with his legs and pushing with his hands, he was able to remove his boots and get the rope off his legs. Standing and raising his elbows, he estimated the rope binding his wrists was still two feet from the post top. Deeply bending his knees, he jumped and hooked the crook of his elbow over the top. The weight of his body tried to pull him back to where he'd started, but he managed to get his left heel around the post and pulled his lower body forward. Throwing his head backward, he wrenched his arm off the post and fell heavily.

As soon as he hit the ground, he rolled away from the heat and once clear he lay for several minutes resting. Afterwards, he rose and edged along the side of the corral until he got to the gate, which had been left open, and went out, following the fence around to a patch of brush. Thrusting his upper body into the bushes, he twisted back and forth until the branches were tangled in the feed sack, and backed out, leaving the sack impaled in the thicket. Now, at last he could see.

Spotting some honeycomb rocks, he went over and sat down with his back to their jagged edges and began to saw back and forth on the ropes binding his hands. Eventually, the strands parted and he brought his hands around to the front. Huge blisters, filled with clear liquid, covered the back of his hands and fingers. The wagon was turned upside down near the barn. He walked over to it, removed a glob of grease from the inside of a hub, and rubbed it thoroughly over his burns.

Next, he went to a flowerbed at the front of the yard and pulled several flat, pointed leaves off the aloe vera plants growing there. Laying these on a flat rock, he beat them with a round stone, making a jelly-like paste. He gently rubbed this into the grease and in a few minutes, the throbbing subsided and he began to think about his situation.

His saddle and rig were lying in front of the stone wall that had been the barn and although they were singed and charred, they were still useable. Tied to the saddle was his lariat with which he could catch his horse. His handgun and knife had been taken, but his rifle was lying at the base of the wall where it had fallen when he was roped. It had a live shell in the chamber and he had a box of them in his saddlebags, so he was armed.

He knew he'd better act fast before his hands stiffened up, so he went over to the barn and after a couple of attempts at braving the heat was able to drag his saddle clear. Taking his lariat, he walked down in the fields below the house, and, as he expected, saw his horse not far away grazing with another horse and the donkey. He had grained these three just before he was roped. The donkey saw him approaching and trotted his direction hoping for more grain. Scratching the donkey's forehead, he put his left hand over its back and walked it back to the other two. He had shaken a loop out in his right hand and as soon as they were close enough, he planted his feet and made his cast. His loop sailed true and settled over the intended horse's head.

The horse followed him as docile as a dog on a leash back to the house and he saddled up and rode toward a creek bottom to the west. On the way, he stopped and roped the donkey and took him along.

He had to have food, and since everything at the house was burned, wild game would have to do. He rode to a hill over the stream and dismounted. Taking his rifle from the boot, he crept to the brow. Several deer were in the meadow near the water and selecting a young buck, he dropped it with his first shot. With no knife, his straight razor would have to do. It was fragile but sharp, and he had no trouble field dressing the buck. He carried the deer to the creek and carefully washed the blood, grass, and leaves away. He wrapped his slicker around the buck and tied it over the donkey's back, mounted his horse, and rode back to the house.

Bridges dismounted at the front tie rail where the rock walk led up to the burning shell of the house. He put the deer on the clean stones and began to skin and prepare the meat for smoking. He was lucky in a way, because since the smokehouse was made out of rock it hadn't burned. He built a small fire on the rock grill on the floor and waited until it had burned down, making a good bed of coals. Then, he placed some green oak, mesquite, and a little cedar on the bed and the meat on the wooden racks inside and closed the door. Immediately smoke began to pour out of the vents at the top, and he knew it would only be a matter of time until the meat inside was cured. Turning, he noticed a plume of dust and knew someone was coming. Walking over to his saddled horse, he pulled his rifle from its boot and made ready to give them something they weren't expecting.

****

Bridges drew a fine bead on the front sight of his rifle and held it right on the rider's head. The fellow was coming out of the setting sun and Frank couldn't tell who it was but it didn't matter—friend or foe, he was ready.

When the rider was about a hundred yards away, he suddenly slid to a stop as if noticing for the first time the burned house and out-buildings. Drawing his Winchester from his boot, he spurred his horse and came on the run.

Bridges was just about to squeeze the trigger when he recognized Monty and lowered his rifle.

"What in the hell went on here?" Monty asked.

"Hell is about right," Bridges replied, holding up his hands for Monty to see.

Monty swore again, seeing the blisters, and Bridges told him the details of what had happened.

After hearing the story, Monty said, "No reason to stay here. In fact, they may come back to see how you cooked, and they were mighty interested in me so it appears we'd be safer somewhere else. I left most of the supplies at the hidden valley and I think we better head there."

"Well, at least we have something to eat," Bridges said.

Monty said, "I've got the willies. Something is coming and it's not good. Let's pack up and hit the trail."

Bridges had turned his horse and the donkey into the corral and Monty got them out, saddled Bridges' horse, and made a pack for the donkey's back with his ground sheet and some leather strings and rope.

They loaded part of the smoked deer on the pack and headed out just as the sun was sinking below the horizon. Well after midnight, they rode down the narrow canyon leading into the hidden valley. They walked the last few hundred yards holding the horses noses, but when they emerged in the broader expanse, it was dark and silent. No smell of smoke in the air, no human sound—just small animals scurrying around in the grass and the hoot of an owl overhead.

They crossed the stream to the old stone wall and found the supplies untouched on its top. Soon, they had a small fire going. Bacon and pan bread was cooked and wolfed down with scalding coffee. Afterwards, they felt much better. Bridges was bending over near the fire to get a better light while he put on another application of aloe vera when he noticed something.

"Monty, one of these stones around the fire seems to be burning."

"Aw, you just spilled some bacon fat on it. The stone's not really burning." Bridges picked up a stick and raked it out of the fire, turning it upside down. The fire moved up the side and started burning on the top again.

"Well, I'll be damned," Monty said.

Bridges broke a forked stick off a nearby bush and using it with the stick he already had, picked the burning rock up and placed it on another. With a round stone, he smashed the burning one into a dozen pieces plus a lot of black dust. The fire spread and all of the pieces started to burn.

"I wasn't sure at first, but this here is coal. I saw it when we went on a cattle drive to Dodge City. The train that picked the cattle up used this for fuel."

"What's it doing here? There's no trains around, only Indians."

"Well, I hear they mine this out of the ground, so either there's some of it around here or the Indians know where some of it is and have brought it in here."

Both men were exhausted from the day, Bridges more than Monty, and no matter how they turned the mystery over in their minds, they couldn't reach a solution. Spreading their ground sheets and blankets, they were soon sound asleep.

The next morning after breakfast, Monty said, "I think we'd better explore this valley, see if we can find any of this coal; but even if we can't, there's something I've been curious about. When the boss and I found Linda Harrison here, we jumped two Indians riding in. Those Indians were between us and the creek and they appeared to have come in the same way we did, yet there were no tracks, none at all. In addition, after the fight, the one who lived had a broken leg and he disappeared like he flew away. The only solution is there is something we don't know about this canyon. They had horses hidden around here somewhere or there's another way up those canyon walls we haven't found yet."

Monty took Bridges to the last place they had seen the Indian.

"The boss said he followed the Indian's tracks to the rock around this sheer cliff face and they disappeared."

"Maybe he had some friends on top of the cliff with ropes and they lifted him to the top."

"Well, he was already gone when we were leaving and they'd have to have pulled him up right in front of our faces, cause you can see this cliff from the old wall where we were drinking coffee."

The only thing in sight was an agarita thicket some hundred feet away against the base of the cliff. For no other reason except it was the only thing around, they walked to it. At first look, it seemed impregnable. Bridges walked over and broke a long narrow limb off the willows growing by the stream. After peeling the smaller branches off, he began to probe the thicket, first to see if there was any kind of cavity or hole or entrance and, second, to see if there were any rattlesnakes waiting for the small game that fed on the agarita berries. There were no snakes, but on the fourth thrust, the limb disappeared from sight so rapidly that Bridges almost fell face first into the thousands of spikes. Monty broke more limbs off the willows and laid them over the agarita to build a path into the cliff face.

The entrance hole was large enough for a crawling man to enter. Monty approached it and poked Bridges's stick inside but felt and heard nothing suspicious. Finally, he drew it back and stuck his head in and then crawled in up to his waist.

"I can't see a thing. It's black as the ace of spades, but there's more space above my head."

Crawling back out he said, "Let's make some torches."

They picked up some moss from the stream and wrapped it around some short limbs, tying it with vines to make torches.

Monty crawled in the hole and stood up, and Bridges handed the torches to him. Monty struck a match on his pants and lit a one, holding it high above his head.

"Come on in, Bridges. It's big enough for you and me and half the rest of Texas. I can't even see the ceiling." Bridges crawled in and lit another torch and they stood for some minutes staring in awe at the vastness of the cave.

"Why, there's more room in here than there is in the valley outside."

"Hey, look at this," Bridges exclaimed holding his burning brand near the dirt floor. Clear as day a set of moccasin prints led into the cave.

"So this is where our Indian friend went!"

They walked deeper into the cave, and it was obvious that despite the relatively fresh prints, it had not been occupied for a long time. It had a musty, dank smell, and the dust puffed up as they walked. After a few minutes, they came to an ancient fire site. The stones were still in a circle and scattered about were broken clay pots of different kinds. Also scattered were the bones of several people.

"Wonder what killed them?" Monty said.

In answer, Bridges picked up a skull. Its eye sockets seemed to be vacantly staring at the axe blade embedded between them. Past the hearth, they came on two additional skeletons. One of these had a large hole in the skull and the other skeleton had a broken leg bone.

"Looks like they were killed in a fight."

"Sure does. It must have been rough around here in those days." The next thing they found was the most surprising of all—the tracks of three horses, and the horses were shod.

Back-tracking them for a few minutes, they found the front entrance to the cave. It was concealed behind a limestone lip so if you looked at it from the front, it would look like a solid limestone cliff.

"Say," Monty said, "this is where the boss and I tracked those three guys with the running iron. Let's see where they went."

Following the tracks back into the cave, they branched away from the fire site and cut past the small entrance and soon came to a large exit at the head of a small brush-filled draw. Working their way down the draw, they emerged on the back side of the grove of trees across from the old wall.

"Well, this explains a lot of things. Those guys that disappeared were the same three who rode through the cave and took Linda Harrison's money. Also, the Indians we fought probably had their horses hidden in this cave and the one with the broken leg crawled back in and rode away. Seemed everybody knew about this hideout but us."

"Let's go back in and see if we can find any of this coal we were looking for."

They lit more torches and went back in the cave. Some two hours later, they had searched every nook and cranny and found not a sign of a coal deposit. They were standing at the old fire site when Bridges stooped to examine the ashes. Digging around with the toe of his boot, his unearthed several small black lumps.

"It looks like our old friends knew about the coal. These aren't here by accident."

Picking up a long slender rock, he started to dig among the broken pieces of pottery and soon unearthed a small pile of the same black rocks.

"How'd you know to do that?" Monty asked.

"Well, it struck me awhile ago it was mighty strange there was a fire here but no sign of wood. Most of the wood would have rotted or been consumed over time, but in this cave there would have been some sign left, so if there wasn't any sign of wood, these people had to be burning something else, and here it is," he said, holding up a large lump of coal.

Going out to the camp, they put the pack on the donkey and returned to load up the coal and cart it over to the old wall. The prospect of having fuel without having to cut or go out and scavenge it was too tempting to pass up. When they heated the coffee over its blue flame, they were amazed how little it took to provide heat and how long it burned compared to wood.

It was afternoon when they saw a small dust cloud off to the east and knew a horseman was coming. They saddled up and rode out to the canyon entrance. They could tell from the dust that the rider was headed right for the valley, so they spread out about four hundred yards, hid their horses in the brush, got their rifles, dug in on the high ground on either side of the entrance, and waited.

— Chapter Twenty-Four —

Buzzards Gather

IN A BACK ROOM at the Silver Spur, Linda Harrison stared at Bud Hardin and Sheriff Bosque. Her face was red with anger and her eyes flashed as she said, "Half the crew's stove up, two killed, teeth poked out, cheekbones, ribs, arms, legs broken, noses and faces ruined, and what do we have to show for it? Nothing. Not a thing. He's not hung, not dead. You can't even catch him even though we've got the law and everybody else on our side. The railroad man is going to be here next week and Adam Ballard has got to be dead, and we've got to have a deed to the Rockin M or we'll be out in the cold."

Hearing a slight noise in the hall, she paused and motioned at the sheriff to check. The door was yanked open, but he saw nothing suspicious and turned back into the room shrugging his shoulders.

She continued to stare at them, waiting for a reply and finally Bosque said, "We followed him southwest, but the reservation Apache who was guiding us wouldn't go north of the river. Said there were too many Indians out there. No amount of talking would convince him to move. He said no white man could live out there—if the Indians didn't get him, the desert would."

"Well, I don't believe it," she said. "We've underestimated him time and again. I believe he'll make it. Now, what's north of that river?"

"Well, northeast some two-days' ride is his ranch, so ultimately he'd be headed back there. Ed and Lanny and some of the boys burned his place and killed one of his hands day before yesterday, so he won't be able to hole up there. A little further west is the hidden valley where we let him find you. He'd probably head there first. It's a good thing we found out about the railroad sending that old fool Harrison here to scout for coal deposits."

"O.K." she said impatiently, "we'll assume he'll head for the hidden valley, so take the posse up there and find him. Now, you two get out of my sight. You've bungled this so far, and we're in danger of losing the whole deal. Don't even come back until he's dead."

Bud Hardin and Sheriff Bosque rose and tramped out of the back room of the Silver Spur and slipped through the back door. A few minutes later, Linda came out, turned left toward Horan's, and hurried up the side alley toward Main Street. Had she taken time to look around carefully she might have spotted Molly, her landlord from the boarding house, across the alley watching her leave. Molly had followed Linda to the Silver Spur and had watched Hardin and Bosque come and go. Molly had even crept in and listened to their conversation. She had suspected something wasn't right about this woman and now she knew the truth. But, now that she knew, what could she do? It would be her word against theirs, and they had the law on their side. She'd have to wait, bide her time, look for more evidence.

— Chapter Twenty-Five —

A Little Off Center

As Ballard lay behind the prickly pear, he thought to himself, why didn't I just wad that letter from my uncle up and throw it away; this had been one mess after another. Now, here he was, on the blazing desert, sweating behind a prickly-pear patch, and somewhere above him was a man with a rifle.

His thoughts were interrupted by a voice he recognized calling, "Boss, is that you?"

Jumping to his feet, he could have laughed out loud as Monty rode up in a cloud of dust and Ballard turned to see Bridges coming also.

"When you didn't pick up the supplies, we was worried, Boss. What happened?"

Ballard whistled up Target and as they rode back to the valley, he told them the details of his escape, and Bridges told him about the burning of the ranch house.

As they reached the old wall, Ballard noticed there was no camp and asked, "Where's the camp?"

It was then they told him about the burning rocks and finding the cave and they had decided to move the camp inside. It was approaching dark so they hobbled their horses and released them on the grass of the little valley. They took Ballard to the cave entrance and everyone crawled inside. Soon, they had a fire going and were cooking pan bread, bacon, and coffee.

As Ballard ate he speculated on where the posse was. He knew of only one other person who might suspect he'd go to this valley, and if the posse showed up, it would be clear evidence Linda had sent them. And if they did, it would raise a different question. If Linda was trying to get rid of him, why had she nursed him back to health? In addition, why was she trying to get rid of him? It didn't make sense. She had loaned him money. If she was after his ranch, why not marry him and have him killed? Then, the ranch would be hers.

The next morning, at dawn, they packed up and rode west out of the valley. As they reached the gentle slope of the entrance, they turned right a hundred and eighty degrees and rode up the rising bluff above the valley. By ten o'clock, they were hidden in a patch of cholla some seventy feet directly above the old rock wall. From this vantage point, they could see the front entrance to the valley and both cave exits. They were well hidden, but if they were spotted, it would take two hours for the posse to ride around to their location. By that time, they'd be long gone. They hadn't been watching more than thirty minutes when the first riders came creeping through the narrow canyon. There were seven in this bunch, including Sheriff Bosque and an Apache guide. They paused for a minute and Bosque pulled a red handkerchief from his pocket and waved it back and forth, evidently signaling to someone farther down the valley. Immediately afterwards, they spurred their horses into a lope across the valley toward the old wall. To the south, Ballard saw eight more riders, including Bud Hardin and Ed Seiker, approaching in a pincer movement. Both groups had drawn their handguns, and as they approached the first campsite, the valley filled with the booms of their shots. When they realized the camp was deserted, the shooting stopped, and the sheriff ordered the Apache to have a look around.

The Indian looked over the camp. Ballard was careful not to look directly at him as he climbed over the rocks and around the campfire site, for Apaches seem to have a sixth sense, and if you looked directly at them, they can feel you watching.

After several minutes, the Apache walked over to Bosque, and said, "Two men camp here, left day before yesterday." He then trotted off in the general direction of the cave.

"Do you think it was Flach and Ballard?" Hardin asked.

Scratching the stubble on his chin, Bosque answered, "I don't think so. They were here day before yesterday. Ballard couldn't have escaped jail and got here that soon. It could have been Flach and somebody, but not Ballard."

"Well, who could it be? Lanny said they tied Bridges to a snubbing post and he burned to a crisp along with the rest of the Circle B, so it couldn't be him."

Bridges' still-blistered hand tightened on his rifle and Ballard elbowed him and shook his head no. Ballard could read fury in Bridges' eyes.

Shortly, the Apache trotted back. "Three men camp in cave last night, coals still hot, two men from this camp and one man who came in from west. This morning all three ride out to the west."

"So, they've found the cave," the sheriff mused to himself, then asked, "What's west of here?"

"Only desert and Indians, and no white man can live long there."

"Hardin, what do you think we should do?"

"Linda said not to come back without Ballard, so we have no choice. We have to trail him west. Leave a couple of boys in the cave. One can watch the front and the other the hidden valley. We'll take the rest."

Bosque called two hands over and dispatched them to the cave, and the other twelve made ready to ride.

Ballard and his crew crept back to their horses. He knew the Apache would find where they turned up the bluff, and they'd have a two-hour head start, so leading their horses out of earshot, they rode north parallel to the canyon bluff. They didn't try to hide their trail until they passed out of the dry lands and arrived at Little Saline Creek. Here they rode out into the middle of a pool of water and stopped.

"This is where we split up. Monty, you go west. Stay to the creek until it hits the South Llano and hide your trail all the way. Bridges and I will head east doing the same. When the posse gets to this creek, they'll have to split up because they won't know which way I went. Eventually, they'll find where we left the creek, but they won't know if I am the single rider or one of the two to the east. As soon as Bridges and I leave the creek, we'll split and this'll further divide them. When you leave the Llano, make straight for the ranch. They'll probably think it's me headed there to hole up. Before you get there, try to lose them in all that rock along Cherry Creek. If you do, camp in the canyon at the head of Cherry Creek. When we leave the creek, Bridges will cut directly for the ranch. Again, they'll probably think it is me. Just before he gets to the headquarters, he'll drop southwest and hide his tracks on his way to join you. I hope the posse will follow one or the other of you, or at least we'll keep them occupied sorting out the mess. In the meantime, I'm going to town and try to find out who shot Murphy."

"Boss, you'd better be careful. They'll string you up for sure if they lay hands on you again."

Turning, Ballard and Bridges rode off staying to the creek for the rest of the afternoon. The horses were mostly in ankle-deep water and only occasionally did it rise to their hocks. Just before dark, they found a rock ledge leading out of the creek bottom and rode up on the bank.

"I should catch you and Monty day after tomorrow," said Ballard. "The posse doesn't want either of you and shouldn't give you any trouble, but don't turn your back on them."

Ballard headed toward town. What would he find there? Was there any evidence of who shot Murphy? How was Linda involved? Even if he found evidence, who could he show it to?

****

Several hours after leaving the creek, Ballard came to the main road leading into Three Forks. A plan had began to form in the back of his mind, but it would have to wait until near daylight. Some minutes later, he began to pick up the first signs of town—the occasional barking dog, the smell of wood smoke, a few dim lights, and music from the Silver Spur.

He dismounted, led Target off the road, and walked parallel to it. The last thing he needed was to run into some drunk returning to his ranch. Lucky for him, Lindner's was on this end of town. As he came to the corral fence, he skirted it to the gate and stripped Target of his gear. Draping his saddle across the top pole of the fence, he turned Target in with the livery horses, crept quietly to the side door, and listened. Hearing nothing suspicious, he opened the door and could see by the light of the night lantern hanging above the big front door that he was alone.

Satisfied, Ballard crossed to the loft ladder and climbed to the hay above. He stretched out and was almost instantly asleep.

Some three hours later he woke. Estimating it was an hour before dawn, he slipped down the ladder and out the door to the front watering trough. He splashed water in his face to shock the sleep from his eyes. He took off his shirt and washed his upper body in the still-frigid water. Wide awake now, he took Target out of the corral, saddled up, and rode around the back of the livery and past the Silver Spur all the way to the other end of town.

Ballard was now in the scattered houses of the residential area and pulled into a grove of trees and tied Target out of sight. He waited until it was light enough to see the house with the red trim around the windows. Easing up to the back, he opened the screen door and slipped onto the porch and tested the door knob on the back door. As he expected, it was unlocked. He stepped into the kitchen. Moving over to the table, he lifted the lampshade and struck a match on his jeans to light the wick.

A voice Ballard recognized called uncertainly from the next room, "Who's there?" Stepping to the doorway, Ballard held the lamp up in the adjoining bedroom and said, "It's Adam Ballard, Mr. Hayes. I need your help."

Hayes brushed a hand across his face as if trying to push away the sleep and said, "Son, you must be a very optimistic man. You're accused of shooting a man in the back, you break jail and injure half the local residents, and you say you need my help. You must think newspaper editors have a lot more power than they really do. Well, no matter, go back in the kitchen, and put the coffee on and let me get dressed."

A few minutes later, they were sipping coffee at the table as Ballard explained. "When we first met, you said you had a reputation as an honest man. I need such a man as a witness. I know I didn't shoot Murphy, and I also know that the only tracks found near the body were mine. That means that someone shot him from a distance and I'm betting you and I can find evidence to prove it."

"What do you want me to do?"

"Get a horse and meet me north of town. Just ride north. I'll make sure no one is around and we'll ride out to the murder site together."

"How do you know I won't tell the sheriff when you leave?"

"Well, if I was the murderer, what would I get out of being here trying to prove I was innocent? Besides, you're a newspaperman and you want the true story almost as bad as I do."

Ballard was right because thirty minutes later they were riding northwest. After some miles, he told Hayes, "You tell me when we get to where he was shot. I know the trail, because I followed him, but I never saw where he was shot."

"It's just around this bend in a little valley."

They topped a small rise and a valley that tilted from right to left and opened up before them. The valley was screened on the left side by a small creek and a large pecan bottom and sloped up to some low bluffs on the right. The pecan trees were a few hundred yards below the trail and the bluffs about two hundred yards slightly above it. Obviously, the shot could not have been from the trees on the left. The shooter would have had to shoot upward, and any trail broke westerner would have noticed such a wound. That left the bluffs.

They stopped and Ballard asked, "Exactly where was the body found?"

"About three-quarters of the way down the valley. See, the big forked cottonwood and just past the mountain laurel?"

Ballard saw the two landmarks and nodded.

"It was between those two on the left of the trail."

On the right, Ballard noted four possible sites where a bushwhacker could have bellied down and had the kind of shot that would've looked right. Spurring Target to the right he said, "Let's go see."

They rode to the first spot, dismounted, and looked around but saw nothing suspicious. With his rifle, Ballard lay down and noticed that a patch of cactus obscured the trail. They mounted and rode to the second spot. The ground was scuffed and Ballard's hopes rose as he bent for a closer look, but it proved to be deer tracks. There was a clear view of the trail, but nothing else of interest here so they rode on to the third. This location was a slab of solid rock and although the rock was weathered and scarred, there was nothing out of the ordinary. Ballard circled behind the location, but there was no evidence of a horse or anything else. Ballard's heart began to sink. There was only one location left. What if there was no evidence there? Someone had outsmarted him.

They rode to the fourth location and there was absolutely no evidence. Ballard rode the whole bluff, but there were no other locations that were possibilities. Sweat was on his brow and he could feel the noose tightening on his neck. Hayes' face seemed to have a doubting look.

Grasping at straws, Ballard said, "Let's tie our horses here. Walk me down to the exact place where they found the body."

When they got there, Hayes said, "Right here in this small grove of trees."

Ballard knelt down and could see a body imprint in the grass and bushes and a small amount of the dark stain of blood. It came to him clearly then. A big man like Murphy would have bled a lot more than this.

"Murphy could not have been shot here," Ballard said. "There's not enough blood. Besides, there would be pieces of cloth and flesh and blood splattered on the trees and brush."

Looking around at the small trees and bushes, he noticed a slight amount of color about horseman high in a tree right above the murder site. He reached up to pull a red thread off a broken twig.

"Murphy was wearing a blue shirt, wasn't he?" Ballard asked as he held up the red thread.

"So, he was wearing a blue shirt. What does that prove?"

"Nothing yet, but maybe something before we're finished." Looking on the other side of the tree, Ballard saw additional broken twigs and on a tree some three feet away, there were more. Beyond was a large rock and circling it, he saw some scrapes on top. He followed this direction toward the pecan bottom and saw that several rocks had been moved slightly. Just at the edge of the creek, he found another red thread snagged on a briar and held it up.

"What does all this mean?" Hayes asked.

Again, Ballard didn't give an answer, he just said, "Come back with me to the main trail and we'll see."

As they got there, Ballard began to sort out Murphy's trail from the others. It hadn't rained and there wasn't much traffic here, making it relatively easy.

Motioning Hayes over, Ballard said, "See these tracks? This right front hoof is turned in slightly, and this horse was making deep tracks up to here. Now, the depressions are shallow. This is where he lost his load, right at the site where the body was found. If my theory is correct, when we backtrack this horse, we'll find something very interesting."

Within a half mile, they came to a place where the horse had shied. Looking in the bushes to the left of the road, Ballard found a small piece of blue shirt, splatters of blood, and there was a large stain in the dirt.

As he pointed these out to Hayes, Ballard said, "This is where Murphy was shot."

They were on totally flat land with no place for a sniper to hide and Hayes looked doubtful. Saying nothing further, Ballard tracked the horse back another mile until the road dipped down toward the creek, and there was a huge rock beside the trail. It was about six feet tall and some twenty feet long. On the creek side, they found where a horse had been tied and someone had waited. Ballard reached down and picked up a small black cigar butt, showed it to Hayes, and put it in his shirt pocket. Anyone approaching this rock from the town side would be unable to see the person who had waited here. The story was almost complete—only two more things to verify.

First, Ballard circled the rock toward town and nodded in satisfaction. Then, he walked to the edge of the creek and looked carefully around. Finally, seeing something in the sand, he bent and picked it up. It was a standard forty-five caliber empty pistol shell. As Ballard walked back up, Hayes said, "Well?"

"The way I make it out, the murderer waited behind this rock until Murphy rode up and he covered him and walked over the top of this rock and mounted double. Notice these tracks on the town side of the rock. They're not as deep as these on the other side. His horse is carrying a lot more weight after it passed this rock. The killer then rides with Murphy and shoots him at the place where the horse shied, and we found blood and this piece of blue shirt. Carrying Murphy's body, the killer rides to a likely-looking place and throws it on the ground. Riding over to that small tree nearby, where we found the first red thread, he climbs into it and spooks Murphy's horse, which heads for home. Then, he climbs over to the next little tree, with the broken limbs, then onto that rock with the scuffs on top. He picks his way down to the creek, stepping on those loose rocks, and jumps into the water where we found that last red thread. He makes his way back up through the shallow water to where he started. Before he comes up out of the creek, he washes the blood off, reloads his pistol, and drops his spent shell. This is the empty shell of the bullet that killed Murphy. Notice that the firing pin is a little off center. It makes a very distinctive mark. After reloading, he followed this rock ledge up out of the creek and got his horse and crossed the creek and headed toward town."

Hayes nodded, and Ballard could see Hayes had traced out each step in his mind. After a moment, he looked up and said, "I agree. What can I do?"

"Well, we've got evidence and no one knows we have it. We know the murderer smokes these little black cigars, wears some kind of red shirt, and shoots a pistol with a bent firing pin. Go back to town and keep your eyes and ears open. I want to do some more scouting around and I'll get back to you soon. In the meantime, keep these for me." Ballard handed him the cigar and the empty shell casing.

Hayes took the items and headed his horse back toward town. Ballard mounted and crossed the creek and began to follow the tracks of the killer. The tracks were clear, and it was obvious the killer was convinced he had committed the perfect crime.

— Chapter Twenty-Six —

Killed by a Dead Man

As Bridges approached the Circle B near midnight, a quarter moon was overhead and objects were dimly visible. He hadn't planned to stop here, but he was hungry and the thought of smoked deer meat made him change his mind. Pausing in a thicket below the rise leading to the old barn site, he studied the layout and didn't see or hear anything suspicious. Just the same, he was no fool and figured the Sheriff might have someone keeping an eye on the place.

Dismounting, he tied his horse to a bush and slipped his boots off. He got a pair of moccasins from his saddlebags and put them on, and picked up his rifle and cocked it, and padded silently up the rise. Skirting the corral, he waited at the stone wall that had been the foundation of the barn, but heard, saw, and smelled nothing. That wasn't quite true—he did smell something but couldn't make it out . . . something unnatural. It was almost like the tonic some of the sporting ladies wore at the Silver Spur. Cautiously, he slipped across the open ground to the little smokehouse. As he opened the door, it squeaked slightly and out of the corner of his eye, he saw a dark shadow rise from beside the stone wall. Knowing he was obscured by the shadows from the dark interior of the smokehouse, he tilted his rifle barrel up but otherwise stood rock still.

A voice that sounded familiar said, "I know you're there, Ballard. I knew you'd come here, and I've been waiting. Twice you've slugged me and no man does that and lives."

Bridges knew this was Lanny Weitzel, but also knew Lanny couldn't quite see him. He was right, the shadowy figure worried Lanny, it seemed to waver and float in the dark doorway. It appeared bigger than Ballard, but he couldn't be sure. He wanted to see the pale white and pinched mouth of fear on his face. His hands hovered over the pearl handles of twin pistols, fingers flexing nervously. He had only to bend his elbows and his guns would flash into his hands.

"Speak or I gun you down where you stand." Lanny's blood lust began to boil. He wanted to feel the pistols buck in his hands, hear the bullets breaking bones, see this nameless shadow on its knees, smell the raw blood and gunpowder, and he laughed madly at the thought.

Bridges had been undecided whether to duck into the shadows and disappear or fight it out. Lanny's depraved laugh made up his mind. This was the leader of the pack that had burned and beat him.

Suddenly, Lanny's hands dipped, slapping his guns out. As they were rising, he felt a sledgehammer blow to his chest, immediately followed by the thunder of Bridges' fifty-two caliber rifle. Lanny's feet flew off the ground and he was hurled backward until he hit the ground a jarring blow. He tried to lift his guns, but when he got his hands up they were empty. Confused, he tried to speak. His brain was clear, but he could taste blood in his mouth and knew he'd been badly wounded. The shadow moved toward him, but he was powerless to do anything. As it stepped out into the dim light of the moon, he recognized Bridges and started to laugh, but died before he could, with his last thought being, here lies Lanny Weitzel killed by a dead man.

Bridges stood over the body for a few moment. As he smelled the cheap bay rum Lanny was wearing, he had no regrets. This man had tortured him, left him to burn to death, and would surely have killed him tonight if he could. He got what he deserved. He had been fast, but not fast enough to beat someone shooting a cocked and leveled rifle from the hip.

No matter, Bridges thought, as he popped a piece of deer meat into his mouth. Just one less rattlesnake to deal with.

— Chapter Twenty-Seven —

The Texas Rangers

As Hayes rode back into town, he had a feeling things were getting out of hand. He found himself aligned with Ballard, who it seemed had right on his side but very few friends, especially if you didn't count hired hands and women. On the opposite side was arrayed some of the toughest men in the state, such as Hardin, Sieker, Weitzel, the rest of the Rockin M crew, the sheriff, probably the banker, and Lord knows who else. If the evidence were true, they had already killed and would do it again to get whatever they were after. Newspapermen are accustomed to supporting the underdog, but even they have to blend reason with ideals. Ballard was clearly innocent of Murphy's murder, and maybe his uncle had been murdered as he said, but Hayes would have to be very careful or he would wind up being drummed out of here, or worse.

As he entered town, he made up his mind. Instead of riding directly to the newspaper office, he turned toward the Western Union office. Passing the Frontier, he noticed a stranger on the porch. He was leaning back against the wall and his large, flat-brimmed white hat was pulled down over his darting, hawk-like eyes. His knee-high shop-made boots were cut round at the top and were worn over his pant legs. His features were angular and hard. As Hayes passed, the tall stranger took the cigarette from his lips, tossed it into the roadside dirt, and nodded in a civil manner. Hayes returned the nod as he dismounted and tied his horse to the Western Union front rail. As the editor crossed the boardwalk, he noticed the stranger was heavily armed, with two pistols and a bone-handled knife. His clothing and equipment was worn but clean and well maintained. He didn't have the look of a gun slick or hired killer, but he did look as tough as horseshoe nails.

Bob Jenkins, the telegraph operator, was behind the counter as Hayes entered. They exchanged greetings and Hayes picked up a blank form and began to compose his telegram. It began, "Major John B. Jones Stop Commander Frontier Battalion Stop Texas Rangers Menardville Stop." After he finished writing, he handed it to Jenkins, who read it, looked up into Hayes' eyes for a moment, but then without comment took his seat and tapped out the message on the telegraph key. When he finished, he rose and put the telegraph pad back on the counter in front of Hayes.

Knowing Jenkins was the town gossip and having a newspaperman's curiosity, Hayes asked, "Know who the stranger is on the porch of the Frontier?"

"No, I don't know, but he came into town with a city-type feller wearing a suit and driving a hack. The stranger was on a big rangy bay horse. Harry Lindner was by while ago and allowed how the hack was rented from a livery over to Calvert, and the horse had a brand he didn't recognize but thought it was from a ranch near Lampasas."

"They're both staying at the Frontier, been there since noon. The tall one's been on the porch for the last hour or so. Hasn't talked to anybody. Maude over to the hotel dining room says while they were having lunch, they talked mostly about weather and range conditions. Seems the tall one has a brother down in San Antonio. She says the city fellow isn't a drummer because he has no merchandise cases. I've thought it over and figger they're probably from the Federal Land Office. The tall one is the guide and the city man is the agent. They're probably here to make sure our homestead filings are legal. I figure the agent came to Calvert on the train and hired the tall one and the hack to come over here. Now, that tall one doesn't chew. I offered him a plug earlier, but he smoked eight or ten cigarettes in the last hour, and the shorter one smells like Mrs. Jenkins' flower garden."

For the last minute or so, Hayes had been fidgeting, remembering now why he hated to ask Jenkins a question. Once he got started talking, ninety-nine percent of what he said was useless. Most Texans were not talkative—known as silent types, they didn't like needless talk, but here was a clear exception.

"They can't be land agents," Hayes blurted out, just to stop the torrent of worthless gossip.

Jenkins blinked several times and raised his head and swallowed as his adam's apple bobbed up and down. "Why not?"

"Because we have very few homesteaders, not enough for the government to worry about land fraud. I'd know because their proofs of filing have to be published in my paper. Besides, we don't have a surveyor."

"What's that got to do with anything? Lots of towns don't have a surveyor."

"That's true, but Federal Land agents have to have each tract surveyed to check the boundaries and the location of the improvements. You haven't mentioned these fellows having a transit or surveying equipment, and we don't have a surveyor, so they can't be from the Land Office. Are they staying in the same room?"

"No, Maude said they each have a room."

"So, they probably aren't relatives and they value privacy more than money. Later today, if you get a chance, mosey back over and tell the tall one you know some ranchers who have cattle to sell. They're from Calvert, maybe they're here to buy cattle. That's where most of 'em are shipped from. It could be a cattle-buyer and his herder or a ranch owner and his foreman. If that don't work, try horses. In other words, keep your ear to the ground and let me know."

Hayes knew this admonishment was needless. He knew no power on earth could keep Jenkins from trying to ferret out every morsel of information on these two strangers, but he said it as he walked out the door, just to keep Jenkins from talking so he could escape. He hated to be impolite to someone older, but sometimes he wanted to yell, "Shutup!" Once outside, he almost dashed across the boardwalk to his horse and quickly mounted and rode toward the newspaper office.

— Chapter Twenty-Eight —

Trailing the Killer

IT WAS IN A small draw leading down to the open flats that sprawled around Three Forks where Ballard noticed the disturbed earth. At first he thought it was just a coincidence, the tracks he was following being so close to where a badger had been digging. But then, he noticed the rocks, which at first looked natural, had actually been moved to cover part of the dug area.

He dismounted, dropped Target's reins, and moved several of the flat rocks out of the way. He picked up a medium-sized stick and gouged the dirt and there it was: a solid red shirt. It was darkly stained with blood down the front and he had no doubt it was the one the murderer had worn. There was something about it that was strange. Then it came to him: It wasn't a shirt you'd see a cowhand wear—maybe a red plaid but never a solid red. This meant he'd have to rethink his murder suspects, because if he wasn't a cowhand, he didn't work at the Rockin M. He picked the shirt up and carefully stuffed it into his saddlebags, then walked over and replaced the rocks, after which he broke a small tree limb off and brushed the dirt, erasing all signs of his digging. As he led Target up the draw, he brushed out their coming and going tracks. It was unlikely the murderer would be checking around here but no use warning him if he did.

Ballard paused to rest for a minute. Across the flats, he could see the roofs of the buildings of Three Forks. He followed the tracks to the main road where he lost them in the traffic. There was nothing more he could do here. He couldn't go into town and even if he could, he didn't have the evidence to recognize the man he was after.

He rode east toward his rendezvous with Monty and Bridges. An hour later found him on a dim game trail along a brush covered ridge. He heard talking. Not being sure where it was coming from, he eased off the trail into a heavy grove of trees.

A few minutes later three riders passed below him. All he could see was the tops of their hats, and he heard, "He's got to be somewhere."

They could have been talking about anyone, even a bull, but being a hunted man made him suspicious. Could the posse have split up? Maybe when they couldn't find him, they separated to cover more ground. If so, he'd have to be more careful because twenty men scattered are harder to avoid than twenty men together.

The wind was blowing and he didn't smell the smoke until he slid off a little bank and almost rode over a camp fire. At the same moment he heard, "Charlie, is that you?"

Ballard's spurs hit Target's flanks and in two mighty bounds he was across the little clearing, going full tilt. He ducked his head to avoid the slapping branches on the other side but not before he saw two men jumping back from the fire, throwing coffee cups in the air and crawling in terror to avoid Target's hooves. A wild shot rattled through the treetops and then another. Riding up the slope of a small hill, Ballard cut around its side just below the ridge line. Eventually, this ridge intersected a larger one and he cut directly across the top. On the opposite side, he came to a patch of solid rock leading down to a stream. He pulled to a stop, dismounted, and led Target parallel to the stream on the hard surface. After covering a hundred yards, they reached a thicket of dryland willows. Moving back out of sight, Ballard held Target's nose and waited.

It was only a matter of minutes until he heard them coming. He reached out to part the willows and saw five riders sweep down to the creek.

"He must of gone downstream. There's no mud in the water. If he'd gone upstream, the water would still be cloudy."

"Not necessarily. These streams have rocky bottoms. There's probably no mud to disturb." "Maybe you're right. Anyway, we can't risk losing him. If we want the $5,000, we're going to have to cover all the angles."

"O.K., Bobby, you and Jack take the upstream side and the rest of us will head on downstream. The first one who finds where he left the stream, fires his pistol twice, and the others will come running."

With this, they rode off in either direction, Bobby and Jack passing just below Ballard as they headed upstream. After they were well gone, he took his hand off Target's nose, remounted, and rode off the rocks in the direction he had originally come from. So, there was a $5,000 dollar reward for him! Who posted it? They must be getting desperate. Every owlhoot in the area would be out trying to collect.

As Ballard reached their camp, he dismounted. The coffee pot was still hot so he helped himself to a cup. There was also some cooked bacon and a few biscuits in a skillet. He ate it all then gathered up their bedrolls and anything else that would burn and dropped it on the fire. The coals were still hot and it was only a matter of minutes before it flamed up. Once it was burning, he mounted and turned due west. Looking back, he could see the fire was making a dark smoke. The smoke didn't worry Ballard much because it was approaching dark, just at that hazy twilight of the day. Even if they saw it and doubled back, he'd escape in the night.

The dying glow of the sun mixed with the brown and tan earth tones of the surrounding land. Small herds of deer broke and trotted off as he approached. Twice he saw coyotes and once a bobcat in the distance. Quail were calling and he saw several dove hurrying to get a drink before going to roost.

Whang! The bullet ricocheted off a nearby rock. Slapping Target with his hand, they were off in the scattered brush. The land here was relatively flat and Ballard looked back over his shoulder as another bullet hummed over his head and kicked up dirt ahead. Boom! Another shot, this time striking to his right. He heeled Target hard to the left because it seemed the shooter had the range. Another shot roared past, but it wasn't as close as the others. This time, as Ballard looked back, he picked them up on the crown of the ridge. Two men, dead still, on horseback, taking pot shots. That explained how they were getting so close. Ballard knew if the shooters had been riding, they wouldn't have been so accurate. No matter, he thought, we're out of range now, as he rode into a dry wash. The shooters took their chances by stopping, and they lost. He gave Target his head, and he ate up the bottom of that wash like a lion on prime beef.

They covered a mile flat out and hit a slight upgrade leading into a draw. Up the draw, and into some brush below a rising ridge, they cut a long half circle around some scrub oaks and Ballard drew up to blow Target. Dark had already won its struggle with twilight on the flats below, but he could hear the shooters thrashing around and cussing in the wash. Knowing they'd never pick up his trail in the dark, he eased Target on around the crown of the hill, rode off the other side, and continued toward the ranch.

It was after midnight when Ballard reached the vicinity of the burned-out headquarters. Monty and Bridges were some twelve miles farther on, camped in the old box canyon where they had penned the cattle before the trail drive, but something made Ballard pull up here. As he tied Target to a bush, it came to him what it was: He was tired of running, tired of being chased. If someone were here watching for him, they had just drawn a black bean, Ballard thought as he drew his Bowie knife from its sheath and felt its razor-sharp blade. Taking off his shell belt and holster, he hung them over the saddlehorn but stuck the pistol down the front of his pants. Cautiously, he made his way up the rise to the back of the corral. He dropped to his hands and knees and crawled under the bottom rail of the corral. Rising on the other side, he slipped down the side of the pole fence to the front gate. The half moon was obscured by clouds, and it was pitch black.

After a pause, he was satisfied there was no one on this side of the yard. If they were waiting, it was somewhere around the burned house. Angling to the left along the dark shadows of the remains of the barn, he got as close to the house as he could and cut directly across to the nearest cottonwood tree. As he stepped over the low rock wall around the yard, he tripped and fell on a mound—a mound that hadn't been here before. A mound exactly the right size for a grave. The hair on his neck crawled. Who was buried here? It seemed it had to be Monty or Bridges. If someone had been killed from the posse, they'd have taken him home to bury.

He hurried back to Target, anxious to get to Cherry Creek and see what had happened here. Just before daylight, Ballard topped the rise leading down to the entrance to the box canyon. He could see someone below feeding wood into a fire. There was only one person and he wondered which it would be. Spurring Target, Ballard headed down the slope with a heavy heart to hear the bad news.

— Chapter Twenty-Nine —

The Kidnapping of Virginia Murphy

VIRGINIA MURPHY WAS UP well before first light. She dressed quietly in the dark. Outside in the ranch yard she could hear the crew coming awake. She hadn't really admitted to herself why she was dressing in the dark, but she had an uneasy feeling since her dad was shot, almost like she was being held prisoner on her own land. Hardin, under the cover of providing for her protection while "outlaws were on the loose," as he put it, was having her watched. At first, she had thought it was all right, but now she was beginning to wonder at its purpose. She knew if she told him she wanted to go out alone today, he would give her that leer that made her skin crawl, and say, "Now sweetheart, we can't let you do that. It's not safe."

She had to admit she was afraid of him, but if she was afraid of him, she was terrified of Ed Seiker. Hardin had assigned Seiker to be her guard, which she knew meant to keep an eye on her, and he did literally. He stared at her to the point she felt unclean. It wasn't a quick glance, but a slow deliberate look that seemed to remove each garment one at a time.

She didn't have anyone she could tell her fears to. Plunk Murray was her only friend, and she trusted him completely, but if she told him, it would just get him killed. So, she was trying to handle it herself and the first step was to sneak out of the house. Hardin wouldn't like this, especially if he knew her intentions were to try to find Ballard.

Adam Ballard was in her mind constantly. In fact, he had scarcely left her thoughts from the first day she saw him. She remembered his strong handsome face filled with concern as he apologized for bumping into her. How her heart had fluttered. She also remembered his swift and righteous anger as he administered a well-deserved whipping to the loudmouth Hardin. Her father's hand on her arm was the only thing that kept her from running to his side. His large mournful eyes had drawn her, the rippling muscles under his shirt attracted her, and the power of his iron fist excited her. He was her man, marked in her heart among all others, her man or no man would be. The why didn't matter, the reality was all that counted.

As she and her father had walked away from the fight, she remembered his remark, "Quite a man," and she knew even though they were on opposite sides of the fence, her father respected Ballard. And now, thinking back, she knew why. They were so much alike—strong but kind, stubborn, with tempers, iron-willed and honest, willing to stand in peace or fight to the death over principle.

Her thoughts drifted to the second time they met, in town. Her heart had soared, his tongue was tied, he was tripping and falling around, blushing like a schoolboy. He was clumsy from love and she had been immensely complimented by it. But then came the terrible news of her father's murder and she almost went insane. It couldn't happen! One day he was there, the next he was gone. She still felt his presence everywhere. While working in the kitchen, she would turn to pour him another cup of coffee at the kitchen table, or rush to the living room to see if he wanted a piece of her fresh baked apple pie. She always glanced at his favorite chair near the fireplace to see if he was there and any step on the front porch would bring a smile to her face expecting him to come through the front door. But he never did, and never would, and this was the hardest thing to get used to.

Harder to accept than his death was the idea that Ballard had murdered him. She could believe that Ballard, if he was pushed into it, would have shot her dad in a fair fight, but there was no way she could believe he deliberately murdered him, especially with a shot in the back. Never! At first, listening to the evidence and hurt and dazed by her father's death, she had let herself be convinced, but seeing him in jail, she knew it wasn't so. She had wanted to tell him right there, but the Harrison woman had angered and confused her—yes, she had to admit, made her jealous. Then she had wanted to hurt him, to get even, so she left, letting him think she believed he was a back-shooting murderer. Since then, she had thought it over and she knew what she had to do: first, find Ballard and tell him she believed him innocent; second, fight for her man. No squint-eyed, milk-skinned, city blond was going to take him without a fight.

She rose from pulling on her boots. It would be an hour before Hardin would send the maid to wake her, she thought, as she raised the window and crawled out.

She was lucky on two counts. The first was that her window faced away from the outbuildings, and second, there were bushes that obscured this side of the house. While still hidden, she peeked out; but it was too dark to make out anything, and she reasoned that if she couldn't see, neither could anyone else. Quickly, she crossed the main yard, skirting the big barn that contained the stables. Some of the better horses were constantly stabled, those too valuable to risk injury while running loose, and her mare, Sugar, was one of these. She slipped through the back door and took her gear from the dark tack room, and said a silent thank you to Plunk Murray, whose strict rules concerning proper storage made it possible to find your gear in the dark. Hurrying to Sugar's stall, she shushed the mare's greeting whinny, and saddled up and led her through the rear doors. A faint gray was just visible to the east as she mounted.

At first she rode north, keeping the barn between her and the bunkhouse, but once across the surrounding flats and into the brushy hills, she turned southeast, skirting the ranch. She reached the main entrance road, crossed it, and turned almost due west toward the Circle B. The morning sky had turned pearl gray, and there was a growing pink in the east. At most, she had another thirty minutes before the stabled horses were given their morning feed. If the maid hadn't sounded the alarm by then, her missing horse would give her away. Wanting to make the most of her time, she loosened the reins and let Sugar lope. She was riding through scattered cattle and every chance she got she would ride in one of their numerous trails. She thought this might slow down anyone following her. New calves getting their first curious look at a horse and rider wobbled over and then fled, tail in the air, back to their mother's side. The morning air was fresh and cool, almost intoxicating. It was great to be alive on such a day.

It was midmorning when she arrived at the Circle B. Riding directly into the yard, she let Sugar drink at the spring and then tied her to the rail where the main house had been. She had been told the house burned but had been led to believe it was an accident. Now looking around at the other burned buildings, she knew this was no accident. No amount of wind would have ignited all these buildings. This fire was deliberately set.

She raised her gloved hands to her lips and called, but her voice echoed off the cottonwoods and gutted buildings and died away without a reply.

Walking around the side of the yard, her heart almost stopped at the sight of a fresh-dug grave. She ran to it, but there was no marker to indicate who was buried here. Could it be Adam? No, her brain told her fluttering heart, Hardin or Bosque would surely have told her. They would have boasted of his death. Less fearful, now she wondered if it could be Monty or Bridges? That didn't seem likely either, for the same reason—no one had bragged about it. It had to be one of the posse or of the Rockin M crew, but which one, and why hadn't anyone mentioned it?

It was then she noticed the boot prints leading to and from the grave, and some scuff marks and a handprint on top like someone had tripped and fallen and put their hand out to catch themselves. Curious, she followed the tracks over to the corral, through the gate, and to the back fence. She saw where someone had crawled under the bottom pole, and walked away on the other side. Returning to the yard, she untied Sugar and rode around the corral, following the trail to the brush below the headquarters. She found where a horse had been tied and looking at the horseshoe prints, she noted how large they were. Looking further she found several jet black horse hairs snagged on thorns. She was now reasonably satisfied this horse was Target.

Kicking Sugar with her heels, she struck out at a trot, following the horse west. It was approaching sundown when she topped a rise and saw two men at a campfire below. She couldn't see their horses, but the one with his back to her was the same size as Adam and had on the same kind of blue shirt. She spurred Sugar off the ridge.

Riding near the fire, she dismounted and ran to the kneeling man saying, "Adam, Adam."

She was somewhat suspicious when neither man faced her, and her suspicion turned to terror as the man at the fire dropped the skillet and turned, throwing his arms around her. It was Ed Seiker.

"Come to me, sweetheart. You'll like me much better than Ballard."

She struggled, but he bent her over backwards and his lips moved relentlessly closer to hers. His whiskey breath nauseated her and his strength frightened her, but his leg, which was between hers rubbing on her crotch, infuriated her. Of the conflicting feelings, anger was the most powerful, and as his lips brushed hers, she raised her right foot and with all the strength in her body, drove the sharp leather heel directly onto the top of his left foot.

Seiker, uttering a string of curse words, dropped her. Staggering back, she fell and before she could rise, he stepped forward and slapped her across the face, knocking her dazed to the ground. As she shook her head from side-to-side trying to clear the cobwebs, rough hands rolled her over and Seiker said, "Want to play rough, huh? I'll show you what rough is," and he grabbed her blouse at the neck and ripped it to her waist.

Her hands flew up to cover her naked breast, just as a shot rang out and Seiker's hat flew from his head. Breathing heavily, Seiker glared at the ranch hand holding the rifle.

"That's enough, Seiker. Leave the lady alone."

"If you don't like what I'm doing, just wait for me on the other side of the hill."

In reply, the puncher levered a new shell into the Winchester and its barrel never wavered from Seiker's belly button.

"Be reasonable, Steele, why let a prime piece like Miss Murphy go to waste? We can both have some."

Steele raised the rifle to eye level and said, "All I know is Hardin said take her to Cherry Creek Line Camp and hold her there until notified what to do. That's exactly what I aim to do."

Seiker stood for a moment, seeming to weigh the chances of drawing and firing before he was killed. Then suddenly, the anger left his eyes and he turned his back and walked away, saying, "My time will come lady."

Steele uncocked and lowered his rifle. Virginia had her arms crossed over her breast. There was no way she could cover herself adequately or repair her blouse. Steele walked into the brush, where she could now see two horses tied, and opening his saddlebag he removed a shirt. He tossed it to her and turned his back. She was afraid to remove the tattered blouse even though Seiker was still out of sight, so she just put the shirt on over it.

She said, "I'd like to thank you, but any man who would hold a woman against her will doesn't deserve thanks."

"I didn't have a choice ma'am and I'll do what I can, but he's a killer and I may not be able to protect you next time."

Seiker walked back out of the brush and without as much as a look at her said. "Tie her to her horse." Once she was tied, he rode up beside her and said, "Hold still and you won't get hurt."

Drawing his knife, he reached over and cut off a lock of her hair. He placed the lock in an envelope and put it in his pocket. They started riding east and an hour later, they finally dipped down into a little valley and in a thick grove of trees found a small cabin and a pole corral. Virginia was untied and led into the cabin. Seiker lit a candle and Virginia could see it was a one-room affair, but in the rear wall, about waist high was a small door. He hauled her roughly over to the door. She didn't resist, not wanting to provoke him. Twisting the board latch, he yanked the door open and said, "Get in."

He shoved her toward the hole but she dug her heels in.

"It's too dark," she protested.

He drew his hand back to strike her, but changed his mind for some reason and reached over to pick up another candle. He used the burning one to light the other and handed it to her, saying, "Now, get in."

She took the candle and extended it into the dark. She could now see it was a small storage room. Grocery items were inside on shelves and there was no window. With sinking heart, she lifted her leg over the sill. As her foot touched the floor on the inside, she raised her outside leg, and as she did, she felt his hand slide under her skirt and across her thigh to her exposed crotch. Without thinking, she thrust the burning candle right in his face.

He leaped back from the flame, screaming in fury, "You little hellcat. I'll make you beg before I'm through with you!"

He started toward her and she scrambled inside and shrank against the rear wall. But when he reached the entrance, he simply closed and latched the door saying, "We've got plenty of time."

Holding the candle up, she checked the room. On the floor were a couple of blankets and on the wall near the door were the shelves with grocery items. Here she discovered a box of matches, which was a relief because now she could blow out her candle and have something to light it with later. Looking farther, she hoped to find some kind of tool or weapon but was disappointed and about to give up when she noticed a bulge under a stack of old newspapers. She moved the papers and found a rusty hunting knife. Its blade was chipped, but it had a sharp point.

Taking the knife in her right hand, she slid down the back wall of the small room until she was sitting with her feet underneath her. The knife was under the fold of her skirt on the right, the candle and matches on her left. The candle was out and it was dark. She didn't look forward to it, but if they came, she was ready. They'd have to shoot her because they couldn't get her out or get in without being stabbed.

Later that night, she heard a rider approaching and a pounding on the door, followed by, "Open up! Hardin sent me. You got the girl?"

"Yep, she's in the storage room. It was just as we thought. She was headed straight as an arrow for Ballard."

"Good, that means Hardin's plan will work."

"Yep, you've got his note?"

"Here in my pocket."

"Here's the lock of hair. Give me the note. I'll let Hardin know about the girl and then deliver these to Ballard. The railroad man is in town and we've got to wind this up tomorrow. You head to town and let Bosque and Roberts know what's going on."

She heard the door open and close and horse hooves fading in the distance. Her mind was in a turmoil. Why was it important that they caught her going to Ballard? Did they suspect she loved him? What plan did Hardin have? Why did they need a lock of her hair? What was a railroad man doing in Three Forks and what did it have to do with her? With Ballard? The way Seiker was treating her she knew he planned to kill her. Then, why was she still alive? They must want something from her. If it was money, there was no one to pay but Ballard and all he had was his uncle's ranch. His uncle's ranch, that was it! The only thing they had in common was land. It had to be the land. The railroad needed their land for something. She was now convinced she had figured out part of the puzzle, but what could she do about it? She leaned her head against the wall and fell into an exhausted sleep.

— Chapter Thirty —

A Smoke-Filled Room

LINDA HARRISON WALKED INTO Roberts' office at the bank. She saw Bosque across the desk from Roberts. Without greeting either man, she bluntly asked, "You've got the deeds drawn up?"

"Yep, I've got them here in the case," Roberts replied.

"The railroad man is in town, over at the Frontier. We've got to get these deeds signed today," she said.

Bosque interrupted. "Well, we've got Ballard and the girl where we want them. He's at Cherry Creek Canyon and she's in a line cabin west of there with Seiker."

"Good. You two will have to ride out there, get the deeds signed, and take care of the two lovers."

"Oh, no, little lady. If we're going to kill a woman, you're going to have to be in on it. Roberts and I aren't going to let you get that on us."

"You don't trust me?" she asked, trying to look innocent.

Bosque smiled a cynical smile and said, "Sure, I trust you. Just like I trust a scorpion to sting me if I give it a chance."

"Well, if you need me to hold your hand, I guess I have no choice. Get us some horses while I change out of this dress, and I'll meet you in thirty minutes at the Livery. Oh," she said as an afterthought, "you'd better send a rider to Hardin and have him and the crew meet us, just in case anything unexpected comes up."

Linda walked out of the bank and turned right to cross the alley to Molly's. In her rush, she didn't notice Molly's window curtain move slightly. Molly was behind the curtain and continued to watch as Linda approached and as Bosque and Roberts left the bank and headed up the street in the opposite direction. Wondering what the meeting had been about, she walked into the hall as Linda opened the front door. Linda glanced at Molly but went up the stairs to her room without speaking.

Molly got the idea Linda was in a hurry. This idea was proven a few minutes later when Linda came back down, dressed in her riding clothes, and walked out the door and up the street in the same direction Bosque and Roberts had taken.

She's headed for the livery. They're leaving town for sure. Whatever is going on is happening today. I could follow them, but what could I do? Molly sat down in her rocking chair, rocking and thinking, and then it came to her. John Hayes was an honest man. She'd talk to him. Brushing her hair, she put on her bonnet and headed up the street.

— Chapter Thirty-One —

Ranger on the Trail

HAYES LOOKED UP FROM the reply to his telegram.

"You're sure, this is it?"

"Of course, I'm sure," Jenkins said, irritation written on his face.

"Then, it's got to be the stranger. He's the only one who fits this description in town."

"Well, I knew he wasn't no foreman. He's too rough-looking to be a cowman."

"That city man must be from the railroad."

"More than likely. Says here the Southern Pacific requested help in locating one of their mine engineers, and to contact Ranger Jim Day at the Frontier Hotel."

Hayes walked next door, up the stairs to the front porch, and turned out on the veranda where the stranger was still perched.

"Would you be Jim Day?"

"I would, but how did you know?"

Hayes didn't reply. Just handed him the telegram.

Day gave it a quick reading and looked up, saying, "Well, if Major Jones says I'm at your disposal, that is exactly what I aim to be. What can I do for you?"

As briefly as possible, Hayes went over the story of local troubles including Ben Ballard's death, Adam Ballard's arrival, and Murphy's murder. At the end, the Ranger said, "So you think Ballard is innocent, and you think some other people are involved in a plot to frame Ballard and run local residents off their land?"

"I do, but I'll let the evidence speak for itself. If you can spare some time, I think we can clear up part of this today."

"Just let me get my horse from the livery."

Hayes took Day to the site of Murphy's murder and went over each clue and told him what he believed happened. He also took the cigar butt and the empty shell case from an envelope in his pocket and gave them to the Ranger and showed him where they were found. After he finished, Day walked around looking over the evidence, came back, and thoughtfully rolled a cigarette.

Unable to stand the suspense, Hayes said, "Well, what do you think?"

"Oh, it's a frame job, clear as a book, just the way you told it. The question is by who?"

Hayes was relieved but also curious. "You say the question is who; shouldn't it also be why?"

"Normally, it would be, but I think I know why. If I don't miss my bet, it's tied in with the disappearance of a mining engineer and has a lot to do with the railroad."

"Why the railroad?"

Before the Ranger could reply, a rider rounded the bend of the trail and the Ranger said, "Here's someone who can explain the whole story better than me."

As the rider pulled up, the Ranger said, "John Hayes, I'd like you to meet Robert Morgan. Mr. Morgan is with the railroad."

They shook hands and the ranger went on to explain, "Mr. Hayes is the owner of the local newspaper and he's filling me in on some local developments."

Hayes repeated his story to Morgan and when he finished, Morgan said, "Well, Mr. Hayes, that's all very interesting. Now, let me tell you our news. A little over two years ago, my railroad started to plan an extension of the rail lines from Calvert to Lampasas to San Antonio. In the first year, we quietly acquired the right-of-way to Lampasas, but in that same period, the cattle market and business in general improved in this whole area—especially in the Brady- Menardville-Three Forks areas. It appeared if we added these areas, we'd have a much more lucrative route. I went to our board of directors with the proposal, but they were undecided whether the extra income warranted the much greater construction expense. Several months passed and in an attempt to get them off dead center, we put together a scouting and information-gathering trip. We hoped to uncover additional favorable information. In each of the three towns, we contacted the banker because we have to buy land and make cash deposits in local banks, and they would know something was up anyway. We also contacted the sheriff, to size him up and make sure he had the ability to protect our deposits and interests. Other than these two, we try to keep things quiet because the minute the word 'railroad' comes out, everyone raises the price of their land."

Morgan's horse danced sideways trying to escape the bite of a horsefly. Morgan saw the fly, reached down, and thumped it off the horse's flank. Patting his horse's neck to calm it, he continued, "Another thing, we like to do is visit the Indians in the area to see if there's any possibility for a peace treaty. When we visit, we take along gifts like blankets, beads, pots, pans, mirrors, ribbons, and a bag or two of coal. You might wonder why coal. Well, we get the coal from our northern lines and there's not very much of it down in this area. Mostly our engines burn wood. We would burn coal, but it's too expensive to haul down here when wood is plentiful and cheap. Anyway, we've found Indians are mystified by coal. They think it's a rock and they've never seen a rock that will burn.

In the past, it has been the most popular gift among the chiefs and warriors. A year ago, we were meeting with a group of Apaches headed by a chief named Nana near Menardville. They took our gifts and everything was going well. As an ending gesture, I got out a bag of coal and took out several chunks and put it on top of a stump in front of the warriors and lit a piece. Then I tossed them a chunk or two so they could see it was a rock. They didn't respond at all, weren't surprised at the burning rock. In fact, they got up and packed their gifts and left the sack of coal lying on the ground. I couldn't understand it and had the Indian interpreter call their chief over and question him about why he didn't want such a valuable gift.

"To my surprise, he told the interpreter his people had been burning rocks since before the white man came to this country. Furthermore, he knew where there was a canyon with all one wall composed of the coal. Immediately, I was curious and asked him where this canyon was. From what I could tell, it was between Menardville and Three Forks but closer to Three Forks. I asked him how high the wall of burning rocks was, and he told me as tall as ten warriors standing on each other's shoulders. I asked him how long the wall was, and he said he didn't know how long, but it was one whole wall of a fairly large canyon. Well, let me tell you, he sure had my interest. That much coal above ground! But I was still skeptical and convinced it must be low-grade coal, not the high grade we'd need. I told him I'd give a blanket to every woman in his party if he'd send a warrior to get a sack of this coal and bring it to me. He agreed and a warrior was dispatched. Toward evening of the next day, he returned and he had a sack of high grade coal. I asked him where he found it, did he dig it, and he said no, just picked it up along the base of the wall. When I told the board of directors, they were unanimous for extending the rails if we could find and buy the coal. This coal deposit would allow us to fuel our entire Texas lines with coal, cheaper than cutting wood."

Hayes flicked his hat back and stepped down to the ground to stretch his legs. The Ranger rolled a cigarette and lit it with a match he struck on his belt buckle. Morgan kept talking, "Nana agreed to take one of our mining engineers to the deposit and I contacted one in San Antonio, telling him to take all the mining equipment he'd need to test the deposit and proceed to the contact point. He left some weeks ago and that's the last we ever heard of him. A few weeks after he left San Antonio, I got a letter from Mr. Chester Roberts, a banker I had met in Three Forks, which stated he had a contract to buy some land and he'd discovered it had a large coal deposit. Would the railroad be interested in buying the coal? I wrote him back immediately, saying we were very interested and we'd be in town this week to discuss it. After thinking it over, I got sort of suspicious and contacted my old friend Major John B. Jones, asking him if he'd loan me a ranger to help me find our engineer and for anything else that might come up. I was sort of convinced that something wasn't right over here.

"Shortly after I got to town, Roberts came by, along with Sheriff Bosque, and said he'd take me to the coal. 'I said fine I'd like to see it, but before I do, I want to see the deed to the property to make sure you own it.' Roberts replied that the sheriff would vouch for him. I explained it was railroad policy. We never talked business until the clear ownership of land was established. They reluctantly agreed to produce the deed but didn't say when. Today, a messenger delivered a note saying they would bring the deed by tonight. I went out on the porch to tell Ranger Day, but he was gone. Jenkins at the telegraph office told me you two had ridden out here and I came on out."

"This mining engineer's name wouldn't have been Harrison, would it?"

"Well, it sure would. Have you seen him?"

"No, I haven't seen him, but the only stranger I've heard of in this whole area was a Harrison who died out on the Circle B."

"When did he die, and what did he die of?"

"Well, it was some weeks ago. I'd have to look in my records to see the exact date. As to why, it was believed to be natural causes. I don't know the complete details, but I know someone in town who does."

"Who would that be?"

"His daughter Linda. She's been staying here in Three Forks since he died."

"His daughter, you say. Now, that's mighty strange."

"Why?"

"He was never married and I know that for a fact because he's worked for me since he was a teenager."

At this point, Jim Day spoke up. "You say this woman lives in town? Maybe we should go in and have a talk with her and get to the bottom of this."

Some minutes later, as they rode into town, they noticed Molly coming out of the newspaper office and Hayes called to her, "Molly, we were just coming to your place looking for Linda Harrison. Is she there?"

Instead of answering, she said, "Well, that's strange because she's the exact reason I'm looking for you."

Dismounting, Hayes said, "Molly, this is Ranger Jim Day and this is Mr. Robert Morgan. They are both here trying to find out what happened to Ben Harrison, who was a mining engineer for the railroad. Now, we were just on our way to talk Linda because Mr. Morgan says Harrison never had a daughter, and it appears she told everybody in Three Forks a pack of lies. What were you coming to tell me about her?"

Molly told them how she followed Linda to the meeting with Bosque and Roberts and of overhearing their plan to kill Ballard and steal the land. She explained how she was waiting for them to make a mistake, but they had forced her hand because they had ridden out of town and she felt today was the showdown. They planned to get Ballard to sign a deed and kill him today.

"Molly, how long have they been gone and which way did they go?"

"They've been gone over an hour and they headed out the north road toward the Circle B, so you've no time to lose."

Their horses were still fresh. They watered them, and were away hell-bent for leather. They hadn't ridden two miles before they picked up the clear trail of the three riders and set to following it.

— Chapter Thirty-Two —

The Kidnapper's Note

PLUNK MURRAY WALKED OUT of the bunkhouse worried. He had come back to the headquarters yesterday from picking up supplies in Three Forks and he hadn't seen Virginia. This morning he had worked around the stables until almost noon and she hadn't appeared. It wasn't like her. Usually, she went for a morning ride, but even when she didn't, she always came out to curry her mare.

Speaking of her mare, I'll just go check, he thought. As he reached the barn, he heard his name called and turned to see Bud Hardin striding across the yard with two other punchers.

With no preliminaries, Hardin started in, "Murray, I want you, Jackson, and Howard to ride south to that bog on the Llano. Miss Murphy was riding down there yesterday and spotted several cattle stuck. After you get 'em out, drift everything north away from the bog and stay there long enough to repair the line cabin in Gila Canyon. We're going to need more of that grass this summer and I want that cabin ready. I don't know how much supplies are down there so better take enough for at least three days. Everything straight?" Murray nodded, but as Hardin turned to go, said, "You say Virginia was riding yesterday? Where is she today?"

Hardin chuckled and said, "She's up at the house. Caught a little cold. Her horse stepped off into a hole at the Llano and she had to ride home wet, so she's resting up today."

Murray was relieved and didn't think anymore about it as he gathered the items he'd need. It only took him a few minutes to collect his gear and supplies, but when he finished Jackson and Howard were nowhere in sight. He stood beside his horse and reflected on the sorry state of things here at the Rockin M. These two hands not being ready was just one example.

After Hardin and his bunch came, most of the good hands left. Hardin, Seiker, and Weitzel were always picking fights and finally the only hands left were gun slicks. He knew in the next three days, he'd have to do most of the work. Even if these two wanted to help, they wouldn't know how. The only skills they had were six-gun skills.

One thing he had to admit though, the rustling had stopped after Hardin came. For over a year, the rustlers had been stealing Murphy's cattle right and left. He had lost forty percent of his herd. Several times, hands had been ambushed and shot. One night, riders came right to the house and stole several horses. Then, mysteriously, Hardin had showed up in Three Forks, hunted Murphy up and told him if he were foreman and had a free hand, the rustling would stop.

Murphy had come to Murray and said, "I don't like it, but I have no choice. It's this or go under. You're going to have to step down as foreman. You're a good cowman, the best, but if we don't have any cows, we don't need a good cowman, we need a killer."

A killer is exactly what he got. Within a month, Hardin had a crew of gunfighters and had hung a couple of small ranchers, who he said were rustlers (which Murray doubted) and the rustling had stopped. Give the devil his due, he was good at terror, hanging, fighting, and killing, and these seemed to be the only things rustlers respected.

As he reflected, he turned one of his reins over and noticed a weak place in the leather. Better get a spare, he thought, and headed for the tack room. Despite the gloom of the stables, he made it without a light and picked one of the leather straps off a nail. As he turned to leave, he stopped, wondering if anyone had taken care of Virginia's wet saddle. Probably not, knowing this crew. He felt the space where her saddle should have been, but it was vacant. Curious, he reached in his pocket and pulled out a match, striking it on the wall. The saddle was gone and so was her other gear. Still not alarmed—someone could be soaping the wet leather—he stepped out of the room and over to the dark stall where Sugar was kept. Again, he struck a match, again nothing. There was no reason for Sugar to be gone. If Sugar was gone, so was Virginia and Hardin had lied.

Just then, he heard his name being called. He didn't have time to figure it all out so he'd have to string along. Walking out of the barn, he whistled as he crossed the yard to the waiting men.

"Where you been?" Jackson said suspiciously as he glanced nervously at the barn.

"Just went to get a spare rein," Murray said, holding up the leather strap for them to see. "Why, anything wrong?"

He could tell the gunnies were in on whatever was going on, but he acted convincingly unconcerned and after looking at him for a few moments, they must have decided he hadn't noticed Sugar missing.

Howard said, "No, nothing's wrong. We're just ready to ride."

Murray tossed the leather strap in his saddlebag, and mounting up, they headed south. Right away, he noticed one rode on either side and both were slightly behind him. Normally, this wouldn't have bothered him because when he was foreman, he always had the lead, but since he had been demoted, this crew had taken every opportunity to show their disrespect—which meant they rode in front every chance they got. But not today. It didn't take him long to figure out they were hanging back keeping an eye on him. They wanted him in front so they could see every move he made.

As they rode, he wondered what was wrong? Hardin was trying to get him out of the way for three days, why? It had something to do with Virginia, but where was she? Hardin must have had something to do with her disappearance, but what? If she wasn't at the ranch, why try to get rid of me? Maybe he was afraid I noticed her missing and would start asking questions. Maybe Ballard was involved. The way she had looked at Ballard, the spark in her eyes, Murray knew she was in love with him. Ballard was a good man and Murray hoped he cared for Virginia. He didn't believe for a second that Ballard had murdered Murphy. He was sure all these troubles, including Murphy's murder, were related somehow. One thing for sure: he'd never find out what happened to Virginia until he got rid of these two.

Murray knew this area and the whole ranch like the back of his hand and knew there would be no opportunity to escape until tonight or tomorrow. Sooner or later, they'd make a mistake and once he was out of sight, he'd use his knowledge against them and slip away. So, resigned, he pulled a plug of tobacco from his pocket and cut off a chunk with his pocket knife and slid it from the knife blade into his mouth. There wasn't much talk during the ride. What did he have in common with these two? He chewed and spit and watched.

Once or twice when they rode abreast, he noticed the heavier of the two, Jackson, was flushed and red-faced. His eyes were bloodshot, and later when they stopped to blow the horses, he tried to roll a cigarette and finally gave up because his hands were shaking too much. Several times,

Murray saw him wipe the back of his hand across his mouth like he was thirsty. These were all classic symptoms of an alcoholic, and knowing this, a plan began to form in Murray's mind.

It was dark when they reached the cabin and it took a couple of hours to unload, start a fire in the fireplace, carry water from the nearby river, and cook and eat a meal. Murray did the cooking, and as he did, he noticed Jackson looking around the cabin, under the bunks, on the shelves, in the wood box. When Murray questioned him, he said, "Oh, nothing, just curious." Murray knew he was looking for something to drink.

After they ate, Murray noticed his gear had been put on the bunk against the back wall, meaning they were between him and the only door. He smiled to himself. They were so obvious. When he finished eating, he washed up and yawned, saying, "I'm turning in."

Lying down, he was soon asleep. It must have been around midnight when he woke. Opening his eyes slightly, he could see the fire had burned down and it was too dark to see much, but he could make out the glowing tip of a cigarette. One was watching while the other slept. Again, he smiled to himself, closed his eyes and went back to sleep.

He was up just at dawn and quietly slipped outside past the sleeping men. As he scooped some water from the river with a wooden bucket, Howard burst from the front door rubbing his eyes and looking wildly around with a cocked pistol in his hand. Finally, spotting Murray standing at the edge of the river, he sheepishly scanned the horizon and said, "Thought I heard riders."

Murray walked back to the cabin, setting the bucket on the wash bench, took off his shirt, washed up, put his shirt back on, and went into the cabin and cooked breakfast. After eating, they saddled up and headed for the bog. When they arrived, they saw fifteen head of cattle hopelessly bogged in the swampy low ground. Murray pretended not to notice the horse tracks nearby where the cattle had been driven into the mud. They went to a lot of trouble to get me out of the way, he thought.

It was as Murray had suspected, these two weren't much help. To get cattle out of a bog, one person, at least, had to get in the bog and push while another roped the cow and pulled. You couldn't just rope and pull because the suction was so strong it would break their neck. Often, brush ramps had to be built for the animal to put its front feet on so it could get traction. When Murray explained how he wanted to do it, they said, no way. Neither would go in. In fact, they said he'd have to do it. He only nodded because he recognized their natural aversion to honest work and he also knew they were afraid he'd ride off, leaving them stuck in the mud, and they were right—he would have. They did agree to cut brush and work the rope.

By noon, the last cow was on dry land and Murray was sitting in the mud at the edge of the bog. He was covered from boot to hat with mud. He waited until Jackson had released the cow and was closest to him and said, "Say, how about giving me a hand out of here?"

Jackson dismounted and walking over to the edge extended his gloved hand. Murray took his hand and started to rise but pretended to slip and threw all his weight against Jackson's arm, pulling him into the mud. Jackson cursed him roundly as they both crawled on their hands and knees out on the dry bank.

Howard had remained on his horse and Murray looked up at him and said, "Why don't you drift these cattle away from the bog while Jackson and I wash off in the river? Then I'll cook lunch and by that time you'll be back and we'll eat and start on the cabin repairs."

"Who appointed you boss?" he snarled.

"No one appointed me boss, but Hardin told us to do these things. How do you want to do 'em?"

Howard seemed to think for a minute and looked at Jackson. Murray saw Jackson nod slightly out of the corner of his eye and Howard said, "O.K., we'll do it your way."

He turned and started hazing the cattle north. Murray rose and said, "Well, let's get this mud off before it sets up like concrete," and headed for the river, leading his horse.

Jackson followed at a distance. When Murray reached the river, he removed his gloves, and washed them in the shallow water, and put them in the crotch of a tree to dry. Taking the matches and tobacco from his shirt pocket, he put them in his saddlebags. Removing his boots and belt, he washed the mud off, then he washed out his socks. After this, he didn't bother to remove his clothes—just dove into the cold river and started to splash around. Eventually, the caked mud loosened and soaked off. The whole process took about thirty minutes. In the meantime, Jackson, who only had mud down one side had washed it off.

Murray climbed out of the water, he shook himself and said, "You know, what we need to take this chill off is a good drink."

Jackson's hand immediately brushed across his face as he thirstily went for the bait. "We sure do, but I didn't bring any along. Have you got any?"

Murray tried to look surprised like he had only been kidding but then said, "I got a bottle stashed nearby. I hid it because Murphy was such a stickler against whiskey. Besides, being foreman, I couldn't let the men know I liked a drink every now and then."

It was a story Jackson understood and one he wanted to believe. He licked his lips and asked, "Is it in the cabin?" His mouth was watering so much his speech sounded slurred.

"No, it's in a hollow tree down the river about a mile. If we hurry, we can drink it before Howard gets back. He'll never be the wiser and a quart don't go very far."

Jackson didn't seem to want to ride off along with Murray, but on the other hand, he didn't want to split the whiskey three ways. Finally, his craving overcame his caution and he said, "Let's ride."

Murray took the lead as they rode for several minutes before a little valley opened to the right. In the center of the valley was a grove of large pecan trees. Murray rode up to a large tree in the center of the grove with a hollow about head high.

Dismounting, he looked at Jackson and said, "Boy, I feel like I've been on the desert. That first drink is really going to taste good."

It was like waving raw meat in front of a starving wolf. Jackson leaped off his horse saying, "Where's the bottle?"

Murray didn't reply, just dragged a large dead limb over beside the tree and stepping up on it extended his right arm into the hollow. Feeling around for several seconds he widened his eyes, saying, "Here it is." But then he frowned. "I can touch the top but I can't grip it to pull it out."

Jackson stepped forward impatiently. "Here, do it this way." He pulled Murray back, moved the limb, and bent over against the trunk. "Stand on my back."

He never heard the whisper of sound as Murray drew his pistol, reversed it in his hand, and crashed the butt against the back of his head. Unconscious, he fell face down. Murray took Jackson's two pistols, checked him for a knife, and removed one from his boot and another from a string behind his neck. He carried this small arsenal over and put it all in his saddlebags. He walked over to Jackson's horse, dropped the saddle, and removed two leather strings and the lariat. He tied Jackson's hands behind him with one of the strings, he used the other for his feet and used the lariat to bind him to the tree. Pulling Jackson's head back he gagged him with his own bandana.

He walked back to the grounded saddle and pulled Jackson's rifle from its boot and smashed it against a tree. He checked the bags and bedroll for weapons but found none. Last, he walked back and removed the unconscious man's boots and tied them together and looped the string over his saddle horn. Taking the reins of the unsaddled horse, he mounted his own and rode out of the trees.

He stayed to the rocks until he was out of sight, then cut directly north toward the Rockin M. After he had ridden several miles, he pulled Jackson's horse up beside his own, removed the bridle, tossed it on the ground, and rode on, leaving the horse to find its way home. It was late afternoon when he reached the flats surrounding the headquarters. He stayed in the brush on the ridge and rode around the large basin. His reasoning was simple: if Hardin had sent him south and west, then whatever he was trying to hide was north or east. He reached the north side of the valley, cut east, and now was on the lookout, his eyes scanning back and forth.

The ground was relatively soft and tracks showed up well. It wasn't fifteen minutes before he spotted the tracks of two horses being ridden fast. These tracks were heading in the general direction of the Circle B and in a hurry. Why? Riding in a wide circle, Murray spotted the tracks of a single rider paralleling the first two. These were the tracks of a small horse and he was convinced it was Virginia's mare. It was apparent the tracks had been made at different times. Virginia's tracks were made early in the morning. He could tell because the trampled grass had sprung back, revived by the early morning dew. The other riders had come later and the grass they trampled had been dried out by the hotter morning sun and still lay where it had fallen.

From the trail, it was evident that Virginia had not been a prisoner when she left. These two riders must have been chasing her. As Murray continued to follow the trail, the two riders suddenly veered away from Virginia's trail and cut more westerly while Virginia headed directly for the Circle B. Well, they weren't following her, but maybe they knew where she was going and were riding around to cut her off. Now convinced he knew where she was headed, Murray spurred his horse in the gathering darkness toward the Circle B. When he got to the burned out headquarters, it was too dark to read signs and he had no choice but to camp for the night.

The next morning, as soon as it was light, he left his horse in the corral and walked toward the house site looking for tracks. He hadn't gone ten paces before he spotted small boot tracks coming directly to the corral. They seemed to be following or walking with a larger set of tracks. He backtracked them to the house site and saw the new grave. He could tell the grave was several days old and wondered who was buried there. He followed her tracks to where she had tied her horse. He noted the direction she had headed when she left.

He returned to the corral, opened the gate, mounted his horse, and rode along the outside of the corral fence until he intercepted her trail. He followed it to the bottom of the hill. He saw where a horse had been tied. The black horsehair on the bushes and the size of the horse's hooves told him it was Ballard's horse. The rest of the story was plain Virginia was following Ballard.

Much of the anxiety about her safety left him. He was confident she was with Ballard and safe. He decided to play his hunch. He knew the general direction they were headed, so he would cut across and find where they were camped. If he missed them, he could always circle back and follow the sign.

It was nearly noon when he smelled the smoke. It was faint, but someone had a fire nearby. Dismounting, he got a pair of field glasses from his saddlebags and crawled to the lip of the ridge in front. Across the valley, he spotted a small canyon and a faint drift of smoke. Taking the glasses, he carefully scanned the canyon entrance and spotted the camp. There were three horses, saddled and ready to ride. One was definitely Ballard's black stallion, but to his dismay neither of the other two was Virginia's mare.

He rose, returning quickly to his horse. The apprehension for Virginia's safety rushed back. Mounting, he spurred over the ridge and trotted down toward the camp. While he was still some way out, he halloed the camp, not wanting to be shot.

As he stopped by the fire, he called, "Ballard, I want to talk to you about Virginia."

The reply came from the brush off to his right, "Are you alone?"

"I'm alone and I've broken with Hardin."

Ballard, Monty, and Bridges eased warily out of different parts of the brush. Bridges was carrying his rifle in the crook of his arm; the others were wearing holstered pistols. "Step down. We've still got some coffee."

Murray dismounted and Ballard waited patiently as he poured a cup of still-hot coffee and took a sip. Then he said, "You want to talk about Virginia? Why?"

"She's not here and hasn't been here?"

"No, why?" As briefly as possible, Murray told the story of Hardin's lie and Virginia's disappearance.

After he finished, Ballard said, "And you say she was following my tracks directly toward this camp?"

"Yes, she was, but those two riders must have circled around and cut her off."

"Well, if we backtrack my trail we should find out. Let's go."

As they moved to mount, a lone rider topped the ridge. In his right hand was a rifle and tied to the barrel was a white rag. He stopped and they rode out to meet him with their guns drawn. As Ballard rode up, he recognized the hawk-featured gun slick. Seiker wasn't looking at Ballard, he was staring at Murray.

"What is it, Ed, see a ghost?" Murray asked him.

"No, uh, No, just surprised to see you here. Anyway, Hardin sent me to deliver this letter."

Reaching in his vest, he pulled out a soiled envelope and extended it to Ballard. Ballard took it and ripped it open and as he unfolded the page a lock of hair he recognized as Virginia's fell out into his hand. Smoldering rage jumped to his face, but other than glaring at Seiker, he made no move, and finally, his eyes fell to the note:

"We have Virginia, she is good off, fur now, yu and yur boys wait there, we will come, don't leave, or she dies," and it was signed "Hardin."

As he looked up, Seiker held out his hand. "Hardin said when you read the note, I was to get it back."

Ballard sat quietly for a moment, then handed the note to Seiker. Seiker put the note into his shirt pocket, and rode back the way he had come without another word.

— Chapter Thirty-Three —

Virginia Strikes Back

SEIKER NOTED AS HE rode up to the Rockin M headquarters that the corral was full of saddled horses. He counted twenty in all, meaning the whole crew was assembled and ready to ride. He rode directly across the yard to the main house and Hardin strolled out the door to meet him on the porch.

"How'd it go?"

"Easy as pie. Ballard, Bridges, Flach, and Plunk Murray are waiting for us."

"Well, that's two surprises. Bridges is supposed to be dead and Murray's supposed to be tied up south of here."

"Well, I don't know about that. Bridges looked mighty lively for a dead man and Murray was free as a bird."

"Don't matter," Hardin growled. "Cut a fresh horse out. We got a message from town and we're to meet them at Cherry Creek Canyon. I want you to ride back to the line camp and keep an eye on Virginia. If she got away, it could blow our whole deal. We'll make Ballard sign first and then we'll come over and deal with Virginia.

"O.K., boys, mount up. We're riding," he shouted as he stepped to mount his waiting horse.

Seiker led his horse to the corral and stripped his gear off. Taking his lariat, he roped a long-legged blue roan, re-saddled, mounted, and rode back the direction he had come. As he approached the cabin, he got an uneasy feeling. One thing that had always stood him in good stead was his sixth sense. In this profession, one had to trust their instincts and on several occasions, his life had been saved by doing so.

Riding through the brush out of sight, he tied his horse and crept quietly to the side wall of the cabin. There was no window in this wall, so he wasn't afraid of being seen. From inside, he could hear the murmur of voices. He sneaked around the corner near the front door and heard. "Ma'am, I never wanted to hold you as a prisoner. It was Hardin's idea, but I had to obey or die."

"Yes, Steele, I believe you, you're not like the others. You're a ranch hand and not a gun slick. Let me go and I'll speak for you at the trial."

"I don't know, ma'am, he's likely to be back anytime, and there may never be a trial. If he catches me, I'll just be another unmarked grave."

Virginia could feel him wavering and pressed her attack.

"You know it's not right to hold a woman against her will, and you know what Seiker has planned for me. He would have done it already if it hadn't been for you. You didn't like it then, can you stomach it next time? Can you stand by and watch him attack a defenseless woman?"

There was scorn in her voice and Seiker could feel the puncher cringing.

"O.K., O.K., let's do it quick before he shows up or I lose my nerve. Give me your hand."

Seiker had heard enough. Drawing both pistols, he stepped inside. Virginia was halfway through the storage room door. Steele, with his back turned, was helping her. Seiker's right hand gun roared, the bullet taking the puncher in the middle of the back. He slammed into Virginia, knocking her back inside. The cowboy slumped to the floor and Seiker walked over and deliberately shot him in the head.

Virginia screamed in rage, "Killer! Murderer!" but didn't show herself.

Seiker reached over and shut and latched the door to her prison saying, "It won't be long. I'll come for you. Think about it. The more you think, the better it'll be." Dragging the puncher out, he threw the body behind the cabin. Then he carried in a few buckets of water, sloshing it on the wood floor, letting the blood wash down through the gap in the planks. He sat on the bunk, removed his boots, and dropped his pistols, knife, and shell belt on the table. He walked over and yanked the door of the storage room open. Looking in, he could see nothing. It was dim in the cabin, but it was pitch dark in the storage room. He didn't think she had a weapon, but he was still leery so he returned to the table and lit the lamp.

Walking toward the entrance, he said, "You can make this easy or hard. It's your choice."

The only reply was a can of beans flying out of the dark and striking him full in the chest. It narrowly missed the lamp and he jumped back, blowing it out, knowing it was just a woman's poor aim that had kept him from being a ball of flames.

Sweating some, he said, "This is going to be fun. I like the ones that fight."

Still no reply came from the dark room. Again, he approached, but this time with no lamp, and from the side out of throwing range. A can of peaches came whistling out to crash against the wall and roll across the floor. This didn't really worry him. She wasn't very strong and the first can hadn't hurt much—just surprised him. He would take this slight amount of pain to get what he wanted, and was expecting and ready as he heaved his leg over the sill and started to step into the room.

The pain came immediately—not the small pain he had expected but a driving agony of searing pain as a hunting knife was driven into his exposed thigh. It narrowly missed his crotch, and he yanked his leg out in an explosion of fear. His terror was her downfall because as he jumped back he pulled the knife from her hand and it fell into the main cabin.

As it hit the floor, she sobbed in frustration and fear. Seiker laughed, "Well, well, have we lost our weapon?"

He got a quart of whiskey from the table and dropped his pants to wash the deep gash. It was bleeding freely but wasn't very serious. After washing it, he took some flour and packed the wound to stop the bleeding and tore a blanket into strips and bandaged it securely. He took the bottle of whiskey and limped over to the table, sitting down sideways to the open storage-room door. He picked up a deck of cards, drank deeply from the bottle, and laid out a game of solitaire. For an hour, he continued to drink and play cards as he waited for his wound to set up. All the time, he was whistling a toneless song just to let her know he was still there and that he was coming again, sooner or later.

— Chapter Thirty-Four —

A Little Insurance

BALLARD TOOK A FRESH shirt from his bedroll and put it on. As he dressed, Murray asked, "What are we going to do?"

"I don't know. They seen to have us in a box. They've got Virginia and they're probably watching us right now to see we don't try to find her. I'm not even sure what they want, but whatever it is, has something to do with both Virginia and me. And evidently, they need both of us alive to do it. Maybe this will work in our favor. In the meantime, we're not just going to sit here like dead ducks waiting for them to ride up. The note said me and my boys were to stay here, but it didn't mention you, Murray."

Lifting both hands to his neck, he removed the leather thong with the medicine bag attached. Holding it out to Murray, he said, "Ride west until you pass through the hidden valley. Once you're in the drylands beyond, build a fire and pile some green cedar or greasewood on top. Unless I miss my guess, when that dark smoke hits the blue sky it won't be long before the Apaches come for a look see. When they come, hold this medicine bag up and ask for Nana. Nana speaks English. When you get to him, this is what I want you to tell him," and he finished his instructions. "Now, hit the trail. Whatever is going to happen is going to happen today, so hurry."

As Murray was riding away, Ballard turned to Monty and Bridges. "Do we have any extra weapons?"

Monty nodded yes and said, "Murray gave me two extra pistols he took off Jackson," and Bridges added, "I've got two pistols, a Winchester, and a knife I took off Lanny Weitzel. Why do we need the extras?"

"Well, I figure the first thing they'll do when they get here is disarm us, and since they don't know about these extras we'll hide them and maybe we'll get the opportunity to surprise this gang."

They retrieved the weapons and began to look for likely places of concealment. Near the fire was a hollow tree with a hole at the bottom and another face-high. Ballard cut a handful of briars and small limbs and stuffed them in the upper hole, making a platform to lay two of the pistols on. He knelt and scooped several handfuls of dry leaves out of the bottom hollow, and laid the knife inside, handle outward, and covered it with leaves. He broke a small branch off and swept all the signs of his activities from around the tree.

Meanwhile, Bridges had slipped the Winchester butt-first into the center of a large patch of cactus. Walking around the perimeter he assured himself it couldn't be seen from any direction and yet was in easy arm's reach. Murray carried a large hollow log up from the creek bottom and concealed the other two pistols in one end. Then he carried in a large stack of firewood and piled it on top of the log. Everything was as ready as they could make it. Now, all they could do was wait. To pass the time, Ballard decided to heat up some coffee. In lighting the fire, he reached for a match and felt some papers in his pocket. Pulling them out, he recognized two receipts—one from the livery, the other from Horan's. As he started to stuff them under the wood, he hesitated and then pulled one out and unfolded it. Now, he remembered why it looked familiar. It was identical to the one his uncle's I.O.U. was written on.

An hour passed slowly and then riders began to boil over the ridge and down the slope. Several flankers spread out and swept around the camp as if they thought its occupants might jump on their horses and escape. Hardin was leading the main bunch and he rode directly to the fire. Looking carefully around at the surrounding brush he said, "Where's Murray?"

Ballard replied, "Guess he didn't like the prospects of whatever it was you had planned for us. He cut out over an hour ago."

"Thought my note told you to stay put." "It did and we're all here, but it didn't mention Murray."

Waving to several of the riders, Hardin said, "Spread out and have a look-see. Check the brush carefully. See if you can pick up his trail. I don't guess you'd tell us which way he went, would you?"

"Sure will. He went west toward the dry lands." Signaling to two more punchers, Hardin said, "Have a look to the west."

As they rode off to obey, he and the rest of the crew dismounted. Several were holding Winchesters trained on the three.

"What do you plan to do with us?"

In reply, Hardin said, "Take their weapons and search them good."

They didn't resist as their weapons were taken, even though they were searched far more roughly than was necessary.

"Show me those weapons," Hardin said.

The weapons were brought over and he noted the number of pistols, knives, and rifles and after looking over each man's belts and holsters seemed satisfied.

"Take a look through their gear and pick up anything else they might use as weapons."

"Tie them all to that tree." All three were yanked around and dragged roughly to the hollow tree, and tied in a sitting position. Ballard's feet were out in front and his back against the trunk with his hands on the other side. He was tied first, Monty second, and Bridges last, thus his hands were on the bottom with Monty's just above, and Monty's hands were directly in front of the bottom hollow on the tree.

Two punchers returned to report to Hardin, "We found his trail directly to the west. He was moving on like he had a ghost on his trail."

Hardin said, "How far did you follow him?"

"All the way to the mouth of the hidden canyon and after he got in there we knew he couldn't cut back so he must of kept going west."

"Well, he can't do us any harm out there. Likely the Indians will take care of him anyway."

Over the next few minutes, the rest of the crew drifted in and reported nothing suspicious. Hardin assigned trail watchers to the north, south, and east, and the camp settled back to wait on something or somebody. It wasn't forty-five minutes later when the guard on the north trail fired a shot and in a few minutes he and three other riders approached the camp.

As the three riders pulled to a stop, Linda jumped off her horse at Ballard's feet and said, "Well, Adam, don't look like we'll ever reach that preacher. You should have married me when I first gave you the chance. Would have saved you a lot of trouble."

Yep, looks like it, but trouble ain't so bad when compared to a bullet in the back."

"That's true too, and if we'd married, I'd already be a sad widow and have inherited the Circle B. But when you and Virginia fell in love, it blew that plan and we had to make up a new one. Roberts, bring that deed over here."

Roberts approached, pulling some papers from a leather case. Hardin was following closely behind, he drew his knife and reached down to cut Ballard's hands loose but left his feet tied. Roberts and Hardin grabbed him under the arms and lifted him to his feet. Most of the feeling was gone out of his hands and he clapped them together and rubbed his wrists to get the circulation going. As he did, he managed to turn so he was facing west with Hardin and the others across from him.

Linda said, "Now, its pretty simple, Adam. We want the Circle B and you want Virginia back unharmed. Sign this deed and we'll both get what we want."

Stalling for time, Ballard asked, "Did you kill my uncle?"

"No, the boss thought that deal up and he would have already had the Circle B with that I.O.U. if you'd just kept your nose out of it."

"You mean Bosque?"

Before she thought, she said, "No back in town."

This jolted Ballard. He thought one of the people here was the brains, but now he knew there was someone else pulling the strings.

"Well, whoever he is, he's pretty smart letting you handle the dirty work, like kidnapping and murder, not risking his neck."

She shrugged her shoulders and he knew she realized she'd made a slip and wasn't going to say anything else.

He switched the subject. "Why do you want the Circle B?"

"I guess it doesn't matter if you know. The railroad is going to build a line through here. Besides needing the right-of-way from the Circle B and Rockin M, there's also a coal deposit they want to buy. The coal deposit is on the Circle B so we had to have it first. That's why your Uncle Ben had to go."

"How were you going to get the Rockin M?"

"Seiker and Hardin were going to let Red Murphy watch them torture Virginia until he signed the Rockin M over. Once he signed, there was going to be a fire at the main house and unfortunately neither he nor Virginia would survive."

As she talked, Ballard looked out of the corner of his eye and noticed Monty nodding his head yes. Monty's hands were out of sight behind Bridges, and Ballard knew he must have used the knife and both were now loose. He reached out as if to take the pen and ink and saw Monty cut Bridges' foot ties and then his own. The dance was about to start.

— Chapter Thirty-Five —

The Opening of the Ball

FOR SOME TIME, VIRGINIA had been watching Seiker. His face was down on his arms on the table by the empty whiskey bottle. He was snoring lightly and could be faking, but he had drunk a whole quart of whiskey in the last hour and she desperately wanted to believe he was asleep or passed out. If he was, she could escape. To stay was certain death, but if he was faking, something worse might be waiting.

She took her boots off soundlessly and slowly and quietly seated herself on the door sill. As this point, she could go either way, and she was ready to drop instantly back into her room, but he didn't stir in the slightest. After nervously watching him for the smallest sign of alertness, and detecting none, she calmed her breathing and eased her feet to the outside floor. Head up, staring like a startled deer, she watched his inert body as she felt her legs trembling, but again nothing. Her breath sounded loud in her ears, like she had a head cold. It seemed even louder than his snoring.

She begin to slip toward the door, keeping the table between her and the drunken Seiker. All she had to do was pass the table, unlatch the door, and dash through it to freedom. Her stocking feet made a slight whisper on the floor and she thought his arm moved slightly so she froze, automatically holding her breath. Watching him carefully, she saw no further sign of life and began to breath again.

On her tiptoes she made it to the door, her hand was on the latch, now she had to turn her head away, to see which way the latch string was turned so she could undo it. This she knew was the moment of maximum danger and as she held her breath and started to turn the latch, Seiker opened his eyes and leaped from the table like a giant cat. But he over-estimated the strength of his wounded leg and it gave way, causing him to fall short. As he fell, his right hand reached out just as she was flinging the door open, and he grabbed her left ankle.

Pulling her toward him, he rolled over on his back and his other hand grabbed her skirt and with a mighty rip pulled it from her body. She now had on only her cotton panties and he snarled like an animal in anticipation. Realizing she couldn't break his grip, she whirled, stepping toward him and stomping his wounded leg with all her strength. Howling in pain, he released her ankle to grab his own thigh and she leaped back for the door. Quick as lightning, he turned and stretched upward, just managing to catch the collar of her shirt, but her momentum was too great and with a ripping and popping of buttons she was through the door, leaving him with her shirt in his hand.

With a savage yell of rage and disappointment, he jumped into the yard and as he came, he was greeted by the twang of many bows and looking back she saw at least fifteen arrows pin him to the wall of the cabin. Turning she saw the most beautiful sight she had ever seen—Plunk Murray and about fifty Apaches. Crying hysterically, she rushed into the blanket he was holding for her.

As soon as she quieted, she asked about Adam. Murray explained how Ballard was being blackmailed and what had to be done. She quickly repaired her skirt, borrowed Murray's spare shirt, and was soon ready to ride.

They headed due east, one main body with two scouts far in advance. Soon, one of the scouts rode back and spoke to Nana. He listened and then spoke and pointed. The scout and three others rode off, skirting the ridge, headed north.

Nana turned and said, "Ballard and his two men are being held over the next ridge. We walk now."

They moved on foot until the last little bit and then they crawled to the ridge line. Below, some two hundred yards away, they saw Ballard standing in a group of men. There was also one woman. Ballard was facing the ridge and Murray reached in his shirt pocket and pulled the mirror out. Nana said, "It won't be long," and just then they heard a group of shots from the north.

As the eyes of Hardin and his men turned north, Murray caught the sun just right and flashed his mirror at Ballard. This was the prearranged signal that told Ballard Virginia was safe. Now, it was up to him to open the ball.

A rider came fogging it off the ridge and Hardin and the others stepped toward him. As he slid to a halt he yelled, "Apaches, at least half a dozen, but we drove them off."

Ballard was temporarily behind the group and he nodded to Monty who tossed him the knife. Bridges was behind the tree and he stood up, reached over and pulled the Winchester from the cactus, Ballard leaned down and cut his feet bindings and stepped to the log in the firewood and removed the two pistols. At the same time, Monty armed himself from the top hollow of the tree and crouched behind it. Bridges went to one knee and leveled the rifle and Ballard, after waving the Apaches to come down, slipped one pistol in his belt and the others in his empty holster and turned to face Hardin and his crew.

Hardin saw movement out of the corner of his eye and heard the distinct clicks as Monty and Bridges cocked their weapons. Whirling, he was confronted by the three armed men and topping the ridge was Plunk Murray and the Apaches, Ballard, his right hand hovering over his pistol, said, "Give it up or die."

Hardin was an old hand at death and killing, and to surrender had never been his nature.

"To hell with you." His voice lashed across the stillness like a whip.

In that moment, Ballard realized what was coming. The scene froze in his mind. Hardin, Bosque, and the other men facing the sun seemed to be glowing. The cloudless blue sky was a background for the forest green of the desert plants, the yellow-brown earth, and the multicolored horses, standing idly swishing at flies. It was a fleeting instant when Hardin's desperation was pushing them into a hole that would be a grave for many.

Hardin grabbed wildly at his twin pistols. They cleared leather in a flash, one firing into the ground and the other firing over Ballard's head. Before Hardin could adjust his aim, Ballard calmly drew, cocking his pistol on the way up, and as the barrel leveled, he touched the trigger. Hardin was smashed in the chest and hurled off his feet by the impact of the bullet. He felt no pain, just shock, and rolled to bring his pistol back in line with Ballard, but as he turned, he saw the barrel of Ballard's pistol center on his forehead, and the bright flash of orange was the last thing he'd ever see.

Monty and Bridges were both firing and arrows were raining on the gun slicks from the Apaches on the ridge. After his last shot at Hardin, Ballard snapped one at Bosque, but a puncher trying to get a shot at Murray stepped into the bullet and dropped. Bosque and Linda, realizing the fight was lost, made a sudden move toward their horses. They were on the other side of a group of punchers from Ballard and he waded into the group, shooting into the body of one, and knocking another senseless; but as he did, Bosque got a clear shot at him and he felt a bullet tear at his left shoulder, tripping him to his knees. As he rose, a puncher on a lunging horse tried to ride him down, but he threw himself aside and his shot swept the rider out of his saddle. Grabbing at the reins of the riderless horse he managed to drag it to a stop and pull himself into the saddle.

The fight was swirling savagely all around and he felt a bullet tug at his sleeve. He saw Roberts behind a tree reloading his pistol and he chopped a shot over his shoulder, knocking him to the ground. He spurred his horse, intending to check on Virginia, but as he turned, he saw two punchers with Bridges on the ground, systematically stomping him. Turning, Ballard rode over one and knocked the other sprawling with his pistol. After hesitating a moment for Bridges to rise wobbly to his feet, he rode up the west ridge and spotted Virginia watching the fight from the safety of a grove of oak trees.

As he neared, she ran to his horse and said, "Oh, darling, you're wounded."

He looked down and saw a little blood on his left sleeve, "Its just a flesh wound, but now that I sure you're all right, I've got to go after Bosque and Harrison."

Grabbing his knee, she said, "Take me with you. They killed my father and I want to be there when you catch them. I can shoot and I'd rather die than lose both the men I love."

He loved her strength and courage, but he shook his head no, and said, "If I took you, the risk of my dying would be greater because I'd be worried about you. I have to do this alone."

Knowing he was right, she made no further objection as he leaned over to brush her lips with a kiss and wheeled his horse around in the direction where the renegades had disappeared. Crossing the crest of the ridge, he was in open range. Dust still hung in the air and their tracks were plain.

A sudden burst of gunfire from ahead brought his pistol leaping to his hand, but no bullet came near. Rounding a thick grove of trees, he was confronted by John Hayes and two strangers he didn't recognize. Hayes was holding a bloody arm and Bosque was lying dead on the ground, two holes drilled within a hand space of his heart. The larger of the two men was wearing a Ranger star on his shirt and he was in the process of handcuffing Linda.

Both men's pistols were trained on Ballard, but Hayes said, "No, no, he's not one of the outlaws. This is Adam Ballard."

They holstered their guns, and Ballard said, "There's one more rattlesnake to smash. He's the brain behind this scheme and he thinks he's safe back in town, but I aim to surprise him."

"Let's all surprise him." the Ranger said.

"No, he had my uncle killed, he had the woman I love kidnapped, and he tried to steal my land, and it's something I want to do alone. Besides, if I wait for you, he might get word of what happened here and escape. Also, you need to help Plunk Murray take the rest of Hardin's gang to jail. In fact, if you don't get over there right now, I wouldn't give a plug nickel you'd find any of the bastards alive."

They realized the truth of what he said and didn't protest as he turned grimly toward town.

Some hours later, he tied his horse to Lindner's corral, passed behind the Livery and the Silver Spur, and approached the back of Horan's General Merchandise. It was full dark now and he could see very little, but hearing a sound from the side alley leading to Main Street, he peeked around the corner and dimly made out a spring wagon tied to the loading dock. He could see it had several bulky objects in the back, and it appeared someone was packing for a quick trip. As he watched, a vague figure emerged from the side door and began to deposit additional items in the wagon.

Drawing his pistol, Ballard stepped out and as he cocked it said, "Hold it right there, Horan. Your string's run out. Raise your hands or die."

Instead of freezing, Horan dove over the far side of the wagon. Ballard shot, but the bullet ricocheted harmlessly off the dock. The muzzle flash of his pistol temporarily blinded him, and as he was trying to place Horan, he saw a glint on the far side of the dock and instantly threw himself to the ground. The night exploded in the blast from a double-barrel shotgun and several buckshots tore down his back. Others struck his legs, and one punctured his hat to graze the back of his head.

Dazed, he heard the shotgun click closed as Horan reloaded and the sound of steps as he moved in for the kill. Ballard knew Horan had seen where he went down, but he also knew he was hard to see in the shadow of the building. So under the cover of the darkness, he rolled toward the center of the alley, raised himself up on his elbows to brace his pistol, and waited for Horan to highlight himself against the mouth of the alley. He felt the sweat on his neck and forehead, and the blood on his back. His arm began to weaken from holding the heavy pistol and then his patience were rewarded.

A dark shape began to move against the lighter background of the front street. Ballard waited until he was absolutely sure, then he squeezed the trigger. His shot was followed by a savage grunt and the explosion of the shotgun. He heard the pellets strike the building to his left as he continued to shoot until his pistol clicked on an empty shell. Listening, he heard the rattle of breath in Horan's throat and then silence, and he let his head down and drifted into unconsciousness.

— Chapter Thirty-Six —

Curtain Call

THE BRIGHT SUNSHINE WOKE him and as he opened his eyes, he saw Virginia.

She smiled happily and said, "Doc said you'd probably wake up today."

Reaching down, he felt the bandages across his chest and traced them up over his stiff left shoulder.

"Have I been out long?"

"Since night before last. You were quite a mess when we found you. I was terrified, but Doc assured me it was not as bad as it looked. He said you were unconscious from loss of blood, and guaranteed you weren't going to die. He took ten buckshots from your back and legs and cleaned your head and shoulder wounds. The head wound was just a graze and the bullet passed right through the flesh of your shoulder. He said you'd recover just fine and would wake up as soon as you were rested, probably today."

As they talked, the Ranger stepped through the door, saying, "Thought I heard voices in here. Is the patient feeling up to answering a question or two?"

"I will, if you will. What happened to Horan?"

"Dead. Any one of several shots would have done the job. There was more money and valuables loaded in his wagon than anyone knew he had. Including a box of deeds to most of the people's land who have recently disappeared. And of more interest to you, a page he had torn out of the county deed records showing where your uncle bought his land. Also, there was a partnership agreement. Seems Horan and Linda were the major owners with fifty percent, Roberts had thirty percent, and Bosque and Hardin had ten percent each. All the deeds were made out to the partnership, including the ones you and Virginia were supposed to sign."

"What happened to Hardin and Roberts?"

"Dead, along with most of their crew. The few left are over in the jail. Now, for my question. What made you suspect Horan was behind this land grab?"

"What started me thinking was the day of the fight. When I was building a fire, I reached for a match and pulled one of Horan's receipts from my pocket. It looked familiar and as I was thinking why, I remembered my uncle had a line of credit at Horan's. When he got supplies, he signed for it. When I was in there the other day, I charged some items and signed a blank receipt. At the time, I didn't think anything about it, but after I began to study the matter, I realized that receipt was identical to the I.O.U. my uncle supposedly signed. Thinking some more, I remembered Horan was one of the witnesses who said he saw my uncle sign. What actually happened was he had a blank receipt with my uncle's signature, and he wrote I.O.U. $2,000.00 on it, and had him killed. After I decided that, I began to think about Murphy's murder. The only people who knew I was riding after Murphy were Bridges and Horan. When I told Bridges where I was going, Horan heard me and skipped out ahead, murdered Murphy, then came back to town. I followed his tracks and found his shirt—a shirt a townsman would wear—but lost his trail in the main road's traffic. I didn't really put it all together until Linda slipped and said her boss was back in town."

As Ballard finished, Day said, "Well, I guess we've got it figured out, but there's a couple of other things you might want to know. The pistol in Horan's holster had a bent firing pin and he had a package of small cigars in his shirt pocket. Also, Paul Horan wasn't his real name. We found a warrant for one Paul Hogan who was an accountant for the Southern Pacific. Seems he and a payroll clerk named Rodgers disappeared about eighteen months ago along with a large payroll. This Hogan was privy to information concerning new lines, and here's the clincher, Hogan and Rodgers were last seen in the company of Hogan's sister, Linda. Since there's no law left here, I'm taking Linda to Ranger Headquarters in Austin, and they'll unravel all the crimes she'll be tried for, including murder. Once that's done, I'm headed back to report to Major Jones. You and Miss Murphy can handle everything from this point on. Can I tell him I'm leaving the Rockin M and Circle B in good hands?"

"No, better not do that," Ballard said. The Ranger looked at Ballard and then at Virginia with a quizzical expression on his face.

Then Ballard smiled and took Virginia's hand in his and said, "In fact, if I have my way, there won't be a Rockin M and Circle B, just an MB Connected."

Virginia said, "If you're asking what I think, the answer is I do, I do," and she leaned into his arms.

I was born in 1939 in Tarrant County, Texas on the banks of Village Creek, in a house with no plumbing or electricity. My uncle Ruben Gardner rode a horse to get the doctor from nearby Arlington. At the age of six I moved to the small town of Decatur. I was raised around farms and ranches. As a boy I worked at the livestock auction and rode as an amateur in local rodeos. I grew up reading Luke Short and Max Brand. I currently live in San Antonio with my lovely wife Celine and mixed terrier Rio (both are well loved). If you enjoyed this book I have another: <u>The Ghost of Hollering Woman Creek</u> also available and coming in early 2011 <u>Watermelon Seeds</u>. See all my work and talk to me at <u>www.DavidThomasson.com</u>.